Nicki screamed.

For one awful moment she danced a deadly dance with the shadow of death. Then she heard the sound of the footsteps in the hall. Heard the nurse calling. "What is it? What's wrong?"

The shadowy figure hissed, turned and ran out the side door.

Nicki fell to the floor on her stomach, one arm still outstretched, head lifted, eyes on the whirlpool. She couldn't scream, couldn't cry out, her voice completely paralyzed by what she had seen. It couldn't have happened. It couldn't have. No. *No!*

Terrifying thrillers by Diane Hoh:

Funhouse
The Accident
The Invitation
The Train
The Fever
Nightmare Hall: The Silent Scream
Nightmare Hall: The Roommate
Nightmare Hall: Deadly Attraction
Nightmare Hall: The Wish
Nightmare Hall: The Scream Team
Nightmare Hall: Guilty
Nightmare Hall: Pretty Please
Nightmare Hall: The Experiment
Nightmare Hall: The Night Walker
Nightmare Hall: Sorority Sister
Nightmare Hall: Last Date
Nightmare Hall: The Whisperer
Nightmare Hall: Monster
Nightmare Hall: The Initiation
Nightmare Hall: Truth or Die
Nightmare Hall: Book of Horrors
Nightmare Hall: Last Breath
Nightmare Hall: Win, Lose or Die

NIGHTMARE HALL

Win, Lose or Die

DIANE HOH

SCHOLASTIC INC.
New York Toronto London Auckland Sydney

No part of this publication may be reproduced in whole or in part, or stored in a retrieval system, or transmitted in any form or by any means, electronic, mechanical, photocopying, recording, or otherwise, without written permission of the publisher. For information regarding permission, write to Scholastic Inc., 555 Broadway, New York, NY 10012.

ISBN 0-590-48649-7

12 11 10 9 8 7 6 5 4 3 2 1   4 5 6 7 8 9/9

Printed in the U.S.A.   01

First Scholastic printing, December 1994

NIGHTMARE HALL

Win, Lose or Die

Prologue

I watch her racing around the tennis courts, and I can't stand the sight of her.

She took something from me. She stole from me.

Oh, it wasn't an ordinary theft. Not the kind where you call the police and fill out forms for the district attorney and attend the trial of the criminal who ripped you off.

This was a different kind of theft. No police, no D.A., no trial. She was never even punished.

She took something that I needed, and then she went blithely on with her life, as if nothing had happened.

I went on with mine, too. Got up every morning. Brushed my teeth and my hair, put on my shoes, ate, talked, did what I was supposed to do, slept. As if nothing had happened, just like her.

But something *had* happened. Something outrageous. An injustice.

Of course, I can't leave it this way. It's not right. It's just not right.

To balance the scales, I must take something from her.

I must take something that she can't run right out and replace, as if she'd simply lost her wallet or her keys or a pen.

There is only one thing that I can take from her that's completely irreplaceable.

Her life.

And that is what I'm going to take.

Chapter 1

Nicki Bledsoe hesitated in the doorway of the sports shop in the Twin Falls shopping mall. The store was huge. All she needed was socks. Tennis socks. The ten-minute trip from campus and the eternity it would take her to find something as minor as socks among basketball and baseball equipment, roller and ice skates, skis and badminton nets, volleyballs and tennis balls and soccer balls, suddenly seemed like a gigantic waste of time. She could have bought socks on campus. Not the kind she liked for playing tennis, but the time saved would have been worth a little discomfort on the court.

She was due at her first practice in forty-five minutes. Her stomach recoiled in alarm at the thought. Meeting a whole new team, walking in cold, knowing no one . . . her palms were sweaty from dread.

And yet, it wasn't as if she hadn't been

through it before. Military brats changed schools faster than square dancers changed partners. In twelve years, she'd attended eight schools, and that horrible feeling of facing new people, of proving who she was all over again, had, like any nightmare, never left her. She hated it.

She had thought that once she got to college, the moving would end. She'd be on her own then, and could stay in one place forever if she wanted.

But just as she was finishing her first semester at State, Salem University's well-known tennis coach and former Wimbledon champion, Marta Dietch, had arrived on State's campus with an offer for Nicole Bledsoe: a full-tuition athletic scholarship if she'd switch to Salem and play tennis.

Nicki hadn't wanted to leave State. She'd already made friends there, she liked her fellow tennis team members, and hadn't she promised herself she would stay in one place from now on?

But her father had retired from the military, and her parents were living on a pension. A good pension, but still . . . Nicki didn't see how she could turn down a full scholarship.

So at the end of the semester, she had once again packed all of her belongings and left a place where she'd become comfortable to start all over somewhere else.

She was perfectly willing to admit that Salem University's campus was much prettier than State's. The buildings were red or buff-colored brick, or white stone, many of them covered with ivy. She liked the old-fashioned, round globes on the tall pole lamps that lined the walkways, and the huge old elm and maple trees, bare of leaf now, that sheltered the rolling, snow-covered lawns.

But arriving on campus after everyone else had already been there a full semester was worse than entering a new high school, which she had done three times. The university was so much larger than any other school she'd ever attended. People had already made friends, joined sororities and fraternities, and selected activities. She'd done all of that at State, made a nice life, and now she had once again left that life behind and had to create a whole new one.

Still, she had learned shortly after she began playing tennis at the age of eight that the sport was a great equalizer. Once she started practicing and playing, she would automatically make friends and build a social life.

At least, that was the way it had always worked in the past.

"Can I help you?" The clerk standing in front

of her wearing a short-sleeved shirt with the name of the store written across the pocket, was not much taller than she, but he was heavyset. His shoulders strained against the knit fabric of the shirt, and the brown leather belt encircling his tan slacks was in its last notch. He wasn't fat. Just extra-large. Football? she wondered. His blond hair was cut very short and his eyes were very blue.

"Socks," she stammered, "I need tennis socks."

"I know who you are," he said as he led the way to what seemed to be endless racks of every kind of athletic sock. "Nicki Bledsoe, am I right?"

She was stunned. No one on campus seemed to know, or care, who she was.

"I pay attention to campus sports news. Have to, working here. I heard you were coming. Leave it to Coach Dietch. When she hears about someone who can do her team some good, she goes after them. What'd she offer you, full tuition?"

Nicki nodded.

"Yeah, that'll do it. Salem spares no expense when it comes to their athletes. Of course," pointing to a rack of short, white socks, "they do the same for their academically gifted students of which," he said proudly, "I happen to be one." He extended a beefy hand. "John Silver, freshman, at your service. I'm a part-timer here. Helps pay the expenses."

Nicki shook the hand. It felt very different from the hard, callused hands of tennis players she was used to shaking. No football here. John Silver wasn't an athlete.

Reading her thoughts, he smiled. "What am I doing in a sports shop, you're thinking, am I right?"

Nicki felt her face flush.

"It's okay, I get that all the time," he said cheerfully. "But the thing is, all of the athletes are out practicing or doing, so who does that leave to work in a place like this? People like me, of course. Our idea of exercise is draping ourselves over a chair, with a good book in our hands. But listen," he added more seriously, "just because I don't *do* doesn't mean I don't *know*. Any questions you have about tennis or our equipment, you come to me, okay?" He smiled again. "That way, I can live vicariously through you, right?"

Nicki laughed. "Sure. I may need my racket restrung. Can I get that done here?"

"Absolutely. We can put your name on your tennis balls too, if you're into that kind of thing."

"I'm not."

His smile became sardonic. "Well, I'm warning you, some of your teammates *are*."

A stab of alarm poked at Nicki. "They're conceited?" It wasn't as if she'd never dealt with tennis brats before. She had, all of her life. Most of them got over it when they got older. But some didn't.

"Overbearing is probably a better word. But," John added quickly, "most of them are okay. They come in here a lot. If you want any tips on anyone, come to me. I'll fill you in, free of charge. When's your first practice?"

Nicki glanced guiltily at her watch. "In about thirty minutes. I'd better get going. It's ten minutes back to campus, and I still have to change." She grabbed three pairs of white socks and handed John the money. "Thanks for helping me out."

"Any time. Knock 'em dead at practice, okay? I'd love to be a fly on the wall when Libby DeVoe welcomes you."

"Libby DeVoe?"

John rang up the sale, stuffed the socks in a plastic bag, and handed Nicki her change. "Yeah. Head honcho on the tennis team. She thinks she's Salem's Martina, but she's not as nice as the real one. Watch your back around her. Just because she's competitive doesn't mean she likes competition, if you get my drift."

Nicki nodded. She knew that kind. The racket-tossing type. She'd been one herself once. She'd learned her lesson.

Apparently, Libby DeVoe hadn't learned the same lesson.

Thanking John Silver for his help, Nicki hurried from the store and back to campus. On the way she passed a huge, old brick house called Nightingale Hall, an off-campus dorm for Salem students. Surrounded by a grove of ancient oak trees, their heavy branches shielding the house from the sun and creating ominous shadows, the house seemed to Nicki to be brooding and angry. Small wonder that its nickname was "Nightmare Hall," a name that had been born after a suspicious death in the house, and had remained long after the mystery had been solved.

I wouldn't want to live in that gloomy old place, Nicki thought. Still, as she returned to her little shoebox of a room, she found herself wishing again, as she always did, that she had a roommate. But the only room available when she arrived was this tiny single on the eighth floor of Devereaux, a tall, gray stone building in the heart of the campus.

Rooming by herself increased her loneliness.

She had hoped that when she arrived some of the tennis players would show up to welcome her, but none had. And Coach Dietch had insisted that Nicki take the first two weeks to "become acclimated, get used to your academic schedule. I'll expect you at practice on Tuesday, the thirteenth."

At least it wasn't Friday the thirteenth.

Nicki changed into white shorts and T-shirt. Dietch insisted on whites, even for practice. "More professional," she had said crisply.

Marta Dietch was one reason Nicki had agreed to come to Salem. The coach at State was good — but Dietch had played the professional circuit, and Nicki wanted the benefit of that experience.

Not that she intended to play professionally herself. Her ultimate goal was architecture. She wanted to design and build homes. Big homes, little homes, medium-sized homes. Maybe because she'd never lived in a house long enough to feel that it *was* home. But while she was playing tennis, and as long as tennis was footing her bills at college, she wanted to be the best she could be, and Dietch could help her do that.

Nicki's hands were shaking slightly as she brushed her long, straight, dark hair and pulled it up into a ponytail, wondering if Dietch would make her cut it. Some coaches hated long hair, even if you swept it back and kept it out of your eyes.

When she had decided that the view in her full-length mirror was as good as it was likely to get, she reached under the bed and pulled out her favorite racket, removing it from its case with loving hands. Her father had given it to her for Christmas during her sophomore year of high school. It was the best that money could buy, and she'd known the minute he put it into her hands that it was perfect. It had, from that moment on, felt like part of her. It had earned for her a Regionals championship, and then, the title of State Champion.

When she left for college, her father had cleared off an entire shelf of a wall unit in their new, one-story retirement home. The shelves above and below it were already filled with Nicki's rewards for working so hard at tennis. "This shelf," her father said, "is for your college trophies."

It hadn't seemed to occur to him that she might not win any. Didn't he realize how much stiffer the competition was in college?

She certainly did.

She slid the racket back into its case, zipped the case, donned a suede jacket over her whites, picked up her gym bag, and left the room.

Her heart was hammering against her rib cage as she entered the locker room just off the tennis courts. You're being silly, she scolded herself impatiently. You've done this a hundred times. You should be used to it by now. They're just people. Imagine them in their underwear. That always helps.

In middle school and high school, when she'd entered a new locker room in a new school, ready to play tennis, there had always been one or two people who had come to greet her. Always. The friendlier girls, usually the leaders on the team, broke the ice, and the other players always followed suit. At State, the coach had taken Nicki around and introduced her to everyone. That had helped.

But not here, not at Salem. Coach Dietch was busy in her office, and Nicki thought those must be the friendlier girls in there, gathered around the coach's desk, because no one else came forward to greet her. Everyone was tying on white tennis shoes or practicing a swing or talking quietly or brushing hair that, Nicki noticed, seemed to be very, very short.

She was *not* cutting her hair. Not even for tennis.

She had learned, long ago, not to linger in

the doorway. It invited attention. So, taking a deep breath and letting it out, she walked into the room as casually as she could and began looking for her locker number. Twenty-three. There, way down at the end, on the left-hand side. Swinging her racket to make it look as if she didn't have a care in the world, she walked between the double row of lockers to number twenty-three.

She could feel eyes on her, but no one said hi or hello, or smiled or waved. It was like walking a gauntlet. And she suddenly missed with a fierce pain the easy camaraderie of the team at State, where whites were not required to practice, long hair was perfectly acceptable, and the coach introduced new players to their teammates.

She had opened her locker and removed the new can of balls from her gym bag when three girls came out of the coach's office. They immediately made their way to Nicki.

Ah, these must be the friendly ones. They'd say hello and introduce themselves, and then the ice would be broken and the other players would welcome her, too. Nicki breathed a sigh of relief. It wasn't going to be so bad, after all. She should have known that by now.

"I suppose you think you're pretty hot stuff," the tallest girl said under her breath as the trio arrived at locker number twenty-three. The girl who had spoken had very short ash-blonde hair, broad shoulders that indicated a powerful serve, and narrow green eyes that seemed to Nicki as cold as jade.

Stunned, Nicki said, "Excuse me?" as she turned to face her teammates.

"I've read about you. Small town champion, from somewhere out in the sticks where the competition stinks. I always say, until you've played a Californian, you haven't really played tennis."

The two girls with her, one stocky and red-haired, the other tall and thin, laughed. They all had matching short haircuts.

The speaker smiled without warmth. "You've probably read about me, too. Libby DeVoe? California Junior Champion. Two years in a row."

The tone of voice told Nicki all she needed to know. "No," she answered coolly, "can't say that I have." She'd met Libby DeVoes before. They were all alike. If you let them think they could push you around, that's exactly what they did.

Libby had plucked her eyebrows to almost nothing. She lifted what was left. "Really? You must not keep up with the tennis news, then. I personally feel that it's important to know what's going on in the world of tennis."

"I, personally, prefer to concentrate on my own game," Nicki said, turning away to place her gym bag in her locker.

"She turned her back on you," one of Libby's companions said in a shocked voice. "That's really rude."

Nicki turned around to face the speaker. "And you are . . . ?"

"Nancy Drew, Libby's best friend."

Nicki laughed. "Nancy Drew? You're kidding, right?"

The girl's strong-boned face flushed. "No, I'm not kidding. And this," indicating the red-haired girl on her right, "is Carla Sondberg. Florida's Junior Champ."

"Two years in a row?" Nicki asked innocently, unable to resist.

"No," Carla said quietly, "I'm not as good as Libby."

Nicki was instantly ashamed. She shouldn't have tarred Carla with the same brush as Libby. "Sorry," she said.

Carla smiled. She was very pretty when she smiled. "Forget it. You're Nicki Bledsoe, aren't you?"

"Guilty."

"Coach told us about you." As Nicki moved away from her locker, Carla fell into step beside her, while Libby and Nancy hung back. "Coach expects a lot from you. She'll probably assign you to doubles at first. That's where we're really weak. And you and Libby would make a great team. You'd clobber everyone."

"I don't *do* doubles," Libby said from behind them. "Ever. And I'm certainly not going to do it with some minor-league player from Boonieville."

Nicki whirled. "I've played in small towns and big cities and in arenas and parks and in stadiums with ten thousand people watching, and I always try to play the same way. The best that I can. But to tell you the truth, Libby, I'm not really keen on playing doubles with someone whose head is swollen to the size of a pumpkin because she takes her press clippings too seriously."

Someone began applauding. When Nicki looked up, Coach Dietch was standing in the doorway to her office, leaning against the frame, clapping her hands. As she continued to clap, others on the team, sitting on benches or standing near their lockers, began to do the same. Not all joined in, Nicki noticed. But some did.

When the clapping stopped, Coach Dietch straightened up and said, "Well, DeVoe, I see you've met your newest competition."

Libby's face turned as ash-white as her hair, and her lips tightened into a long, thin line.

As grateful as Nicki was for the support, her heart froze in her chest. Because she knew with cold certainty that on this, her first day of tennis practice at Salem University, she had made an enemy.

Judging from the look in Libby DeVoe's cold green eyes, a very *dangerous* enemy.

Chapter 2

Nicki's first practice did not go well.

After living in Texas for two years, she was used to playing on an outdoor court, even in winter, but here, in the heart of New York State, January meant indoor play. Salem, like other eastern schools, had indoor courts.

Nicki walked down the long hall to the huge, domed area, by herself. But when she entered through the big double doors, a tall, brown-haired girl with shoulders as wide as Libby's approached. She was accompanied by a shorter, stockier girl. "Hi," the taller girl said. "You're Nicki Bledsoe, aren't you? I've seen your picture in the paper. I'm Patrice Weylen. Everyone calls me Pat. And this creature next to me waving her racket in the air like a maniac is Ginnie Lever. Actually, she *is* a maniac. About tennis, anyway."

"Hi." The "maniac" stopped swinging. She

was short and well-built and had, Nicki noticed with relief, very long hair, caught in a thick, strawberry-blonde, French braid. So maybe there weren't any rules about hair length.

Ginnie leaned across Patrice to say in a low voice, "We're *not* members of the Libby DeVoe fan club, in case you're interested. Watch out for her, okay?"

Nicki laughed, to hide a sudden uneasiness. "You're the second person to tell me that today."

"Oh, yeah? Who was the other one?"

"A guy named John Silver. He works in the sports shop at the mall."

Pat and Ginnie nodded. "John's great. Anything you want to know about tennis equipment, ask John," Pat said. "He's really smart."

"Cute, too." Ginnie said, pulling open one of two large doors. "If John worked out once in a while, he'd be gorgeous."

"Maybe he should take up tennis instead of just talking about it," Nicki said. "Nothing gets you in shape better than racing around a tennis court. And this," she added admiringly, glancing around the huge, domed structure housing four separate courts, "is really something."

"On nice days," Ginnie said, pointing to the glass roof, "the sun shines in, and it almost feels like you're outside."

"It's great," Nicki said.

But her pleasure over the facility was short-lived as the male faction of Salem's tennis team arrived and practice began in earnest. Tension sometimes led her to play well, but not on this day. As she moved to a bench to sit with Pat and Ginnie until Coach Dietch set up play, Libby DeVoe passed in front of the bench, bending to whisper, "Okay, let's see what you've got, hotshot."

It shouldn't have rattled Nicki. She liked to think she was more professional and disciplined than that. Besides, Libby had only said aloud what everyone else was thinking. They were *all* waiting to see exactly what it was that Marta Dietch had seen in Nicki Bledsoe.

But it *did* rattle her. Maybe it was from getting two warnings about Libby DeVoe in one day. Whatever the reason, no one was going to see during *this* practice session what Dietch had seen. Nicki fought grimly to overcome the tension she was feeling, but it was hopeless.

She messed up on eight serves in eight tries.

She missed the simplest volleys.

She began to hear giggles and snorts of derision from her teammates.

Discouraged and embarrassed, Nicki took refuge on a bench, sitting down beside Pat. On the courts, Ginnie was playing very, very well, with fierce concentration. "She's really good," Nicki commented admiringly.

"Tennis is Ginnie's whole life," Pat said. "When she was a baby, her parents must have given her a miniature racket instead of a rattle. The only reason she cares about her classes at all is her scholarship. If it weren't for that, I think she'd practice twenty-four hours a day."

Libby DeVoe, too, was playing well, Nicki noticed with envy. She had a strong serve and a powerful backhand, and for someone so tall and big-boned, she was amazingly light on her feet.

Just before Coach Dietch blew the whistle to end practice, she came over to Nicki's bench to say, "Relax! First time out is always tough. Get a good night's sleep and be back here at two tomorrow."

When she had left, Nicki muttered, "Well, at least she didn't toss me out on my ear."

Pat looked shocked. "She wouldn't do that! Everyone knows how good you are."

If they did, they were hiding it well.

The whistle shrilled. Nicki and Pat got up to leave, waiting for Ginnie to join them.

"You'll do better tomorrow," a voice said in Nicki's ear.

She turned, looked up into the face of John Silver, smiling down at her.

"I thought you were working," she said. But she was glad to see him. He had warned her about this team. And he'd been right.

"I was. But I decided to come watch practice today. Check out the new hotshot tennis star." He smiled at Nicki, who felt her cheeks grow warm.

"Not much of a star today," she said apologetically.

John stayed alongside Nicki. "First practices are always rough," he said, echoing Coach. "Give yourself some time." Then he grinned. "But if you think new shoes would help, I can get you a twenty percent discount."

Nicki laughed. "I'll give it some thought." Then she added grimly, "If I'd played that poorly when Dietch scouted me, I wouldn't be here now. I hope you're right about first practices being rough. I need to do better tomorrow."

"Good luck." As he walked her to the locker room, Nicki noticed Libby DeVoe coming up alongside him, flashing a smile his way and a look of contempt Nicki's way.

Oh, great! Libby had a thing for John? Wonderful. If Libby had hated her before, now she'd really hate her for talking to John, too.

This isn't high school, Nicki told herself. We were supposed to leave that kind of petty jealousy behind when we graduated.

"Want to go get something to eat?" Pat asked as they entered the locker room. "Have you seen Vinnie's yet? Great pizza. I'm broke, as usual, but I think I can scrounge up enough for a slice or two."

"I haven't been anywhere." Nicki hated going to a restaurant alone, and had been eating in Devereaux's dining hall only when she knew it wouldn't be crowded. It would be fun to eat with friends again.

"Meet you outside . . ." Pat said, and stopped short a foot away from locker number twenty-three. "Nicki?" she said, staring at the locker door.

"What?" Nicki moved forward to join Pat. Ginnie was right behind them. It was her gasp that drew the attention of others in the room.

"Oh, wow," someone breathed.

"I don't believe this," Nicki said, advancing to stand directly in front of her locker.

Written on the door in thick, white foam, were the words, GO AWAY, LOSER.

Chapter 3

"It's mousse," Pat said, flicking a finger through the white foam. "It's hair mousse."

The words, GO AWAY, LOSER were already beginning to lose their shape, dripping into elongated streaks of white on Nicki's locker door.

"I don't think that's funny at all," Ginnie said indignantly. "That's no way to welcome someone."

Already, Nicki hadn't been feeling very welcome, after being confronted by Libby and ignored by the others. If it hadn't been for Pat and Ginnie, she'd have felt like a complete outsider.

And now this.

Everyone in the locker room was watching.

"Was it something I said?" Nicki quipped in a brittle voice. She reached inside her locker for a handful of tissues. Swiping at the melting letters, she said loudly, "I hope this wasn't expensive mousse. Seems like such a waste, since I'm not going anywhere. I'm here to stay. I'm not moving again."

Two girls Nicki hadn't met got up from the bench then and, armed with paper towels, came over to help her finish cleaning up the mess. They introduced themselves as Hannah and Barb, said they were glad she had joined the team, and when the locker door was clean, went to take their showers.

That makes four, Nicki thought grimly as she grabbed a clean white towel from her locker. Four people out of maybe two dozen, who had acknowledged her existence.

"I don't get it," she said as she, Pat, and Ginnie combed their hair after their showers. "Why is everyone here so unfriendly? I know I screwed up out there today, but even before we went out on the court, the air in here practically gave me frostbite. What's going on?"

"It's Libby," Pat said flatly. "She's put the word out that she doesn't want you here. She liked things just the way they were. To her, you're a spoiler."

"And people listen to her?" Nicki asked scornfully. "Why? She puts her sneaks on one foot at a time, the same as the rest of us."

"I think people are afraid of her," Ginnie

said. "She has a terrible temper. And she's the best player we've got. No one wants to cross her. She might quit."

"She'd never quit," Pat said with contempt. "Not her. And you're as good as she is, Ginnie. Maybe Nicki is, too."

"Well, you'd never get anyone who saw me play today to agree with you," Nicki said, stuffing her whites in her gym bag. "If I don't do better tomorrow, the message on my locker door will be in permanent ink instead of mousse."

"Libby didn't do that, though," Ginnie pointed out. "She couldn't have. She came in after we did."

Pat shrugged. "She could have told someone to do it. That's her style."

They did go to Vinnie's to eat. The restaurant, in the nearby town of Twin Falls, felt familiar and comfortable to Nicki. It was just like all the Italian restaurants in all the towns in which she'd lived. Warm and welcoming, the smells of tomato sauce and oregano heavy in the air, music playing from a jukebox, checkered cloths on the tables. Vinnie's made her feel at home for the first time since she'd arrived at Salem.

There were other tennis players there, but none of them paid much attention when the trio walked in, or made any attempt to join them at their table. The largest and noisiest table was Libby's, where every chair was filled. Barb waved, but didn't motion for them to join the group.

"You wouldn't rather be sitting over there, would you?" Ginnie asked Nicki as they took their seats. "I mean, with the bigshots?"

"You've got to be kidding. Did you see the way DeVoe looked at me when I came in? Do I look like I'm in the market for a knife in my back?"

Ginnie looked satisfied. "Good. Just thought I'd ask. Most people coming in as transfer students would gravitate toward the most popular people. I'm glad you're not like that."

It wouldn't do me any good, Nicki thought, and then concentrated on her menu.

They were halfway through their meal when Pat suddenly said, "Nicki, don't look now, but someone's staring at you."

"Don't tell me not to look and then tell me something like that," Nicki chided. "Now, I *have* to look. Where?"

"Over there, in the corner. The tall guy in black, standing near the jukebox with the blonde girl. If you absolutely have to look, pretend you're scouting for a waiter."

As casually as she could, Nicki turned her

head. She was, indeed, being stared at.

"That's Deacon Skye," Ginnie said. "He's in my English class. Brilliant. Absolutely brilliant. The only guy in the class who knows anything about e.e. cummings and Ezra Pound. But," Ginnie shook her head, "he's kind of a loner. That's Melanie Hayden with him. She's an artist, that's all I know. They hang around together a lot, but I don't think they're dating or anything like that. They've been in trouble a couple of times for signing into their dorms late, driving too fast on campus, making too much noise in the library, stuff like that. And Deacon argues with our English prof all the time."

The boy in black smiled at Nicki.

She turned back to her meal. "Why is he staring at me?"

"Maybe he thinks you're gorgeous. You are, you know," Pat said.

"No, I'm not. Anyway, he's not my type. Obviously a rule-breaker, while I, on the other hand, have lived with the discipline of being an athlete my whole life, practically. We'd have absolutely nothing in common."

"Maybe not," Ginnie said, sighing, "but don't you think he looks a little like Mel Gibson?"

"No. But *he* probably thinks so. Now leave me alone and let me eat. I need my strength if I'm going to do better tomorrow than I did today."

Still, when the boy in black and the girl with blonde hair left the restaurant, Nicki watched them go with a mixture of curiosity and disappointment. They looked interesting. The only people she'd associated with most of her life were athletes. Disciplined and ambitious and goal-oriented, obeying all the rules because they knew that would get them where they wanted to go.

What would it be like to know someone who didn't always follow the rules?

Might be fun.

But she didn't have time to find out now.

On their way out, they had to pass Libby's table. Barb looked up and said, "Good luck tomorrow, Nicki."

Libby's green eyes shot her a death-ray.

Nicki smiled and said, "Thanks, Barb." When they left the restaurant, she told Pat and Ginnie, "I have to go back to the mall. I was in a hurry today, and got the wrong kind of socks. You guys want to come?"

Pat shook her head. "Can't. I've got a quiz in math tomorrow and I'm not ready."

"Me, too," Ginnie said regretfully. "I'd like to go. I haven't been to the mall in ages. Too much to do. But I'm in the same math class as Pat, so . . ."

Nicki was disappointed. She had thought now that she'd actually met a couple of people, she wouldn't have to be doing everything alone anymore. Still, it was just a quick trip to the mall to exchange socks. Pat and Ginnie would probably be available for more important things, like movies and parties.

She drove them back to campus, dropped them off, then turned the car around to drive to Twin Falls.

It was nice to have friends again, even if they couldn't come with her this time. Pat and Ginnie were a lot like girls she'd known in high school. Sports had probably taken up most of their time, leaving little time for popularity and dating. On Saturday nights when they weren't on the road for a tournament, they'd gone to the movies together, probably staying at each other's houses overnight, pretending they didn't care that they hadn't been invited to the parties and the dances. But of course they *had* cared.

She'd been luckier than that. Being the new girl had lent her a certain romanticism, given her her share of dates and invitations. Until it was time to move again.

She *had* to play better tomorrow. Tennis

wasn't all she had in her life, but it was the most important, now that she had the scholarship. How patient could Coach Dietch be? How many chances would she give a newcomer?

More than the other players were willing to give, apparently.

She was almost to Twin Falls when the car began pulling sharply to the left, and an unmistakable thunking sound came from the left rear side.

Nicki groaned. It was cold and dark out, and the last thing she wanted to do was change a tire on the side of the highway. The car wasn't new, but all four tires were. Her father had insisted on that. How could one have gone flat already?

Sighing in annoyance, she pulled the car to a stop on the shoulder, and got out. It really *was* cold, and the sky overhead was thick with dark, gray clouds. Snow. Great. It was on nights like this that she missed Texas, where they had moved when she was sixteen. It almost never got this cold there.

Checking for traffic, which was moderately heavy on the highway, she walked around to the offending tire. Bent to inspect it. And reeled back, her mouth open in disbelief.

Because even someone with a limited knowledge of cars and tires could see that the tire had not gone flat all by itself. Nor had she run over a nail or a piece of glass. There was no nail; there was no glass.

What there was, though, was a thick, six-inch-long slice in the rubber, separating it, that cried out the truth to Nicki.

The tire had been deliberately slashed.

Chapter 4

Unnerved by the sight of the ruined tire and the cars whizzing past perilously close to her, Nicki climbed back into the car, trying to clear her head enough to decide on a course of action.

She was having trouble digesting the idea that someone had deliberately slashed her tire. It was too frightening. It made her feel unprotected and threatened. The notion that a stranger had destroyed something that belonged to her while she was sitting peacefully in a restaurant, eating, was so wrong, so crazy, that she couldn't quite take it in. Had it really happened that way? Wasn't there some way it could have been accidental?

No, there wasn't. Not a slash that size.

Nicki didn't know what to do.

She could change the tire. She'd done it before. But the shoulder of the road wasn't wide enough for her to work safely. It might be smarter to lock the car and hike the rest of the way into town to find a garage.

She was about to do just that when bright headlights hit her rearview mirror, blinding her. A car had pulled up behind her, and someone was getting out. Two someones. Guy. Girl. Approaching her car on the driver's side. She could see them in her sideview mirror. They walked confidently, as if unaware of any danger from passing cars. As if they were saying, Who would dare hit us?

As they drew closer, Nicki remembered the rules about highway safety that had been drummed into her by her parents when she first got her license. If you're stranded on the highway and a stranger offers to help, ask him to go to the nearest garage and send help. Do not get into a stranger's car. Do not let him into yours.

Good advice. But did she really want to sit here alone on the highway in this cold, disabled car if someone offered her a ride into town? No, she did not.

She rolled the window down.

"I'm not even going to comment on the fact that you've got a flat tire," the boy in black from Vinnie's said, leaning down to speak to her. "And I'm not going to make the politically incorrect assumption that you can't change it because you're female. I'm going to assume that you can, but I'm going to suggest that you don't because it isn't safe right here, okay? We'll give you a ride into town to a garage. I'm Deacon Skye, and this is Mel Hayden," gesturing toward the girl standing beside him. "We ride around all night rescuing stranded travelers, so don't think we're doing you any special favor."

"Hi, Nicki," the girl said, smiling. She was almost as tall as Deacon, and very thin, with long, wavy blonde hair. "Come on, we'll take you to Rif's. He does good work and he doesn't charge college students their entire monthly allowance."

The fact that the girl knew her name made Nicki feel less like she was dealing with strangers. And both of her rescuers were students at Salem, which gave them something in common.

"You know who I am?" she said as she climbed out of the car, rolling up the window and locking the door.

Melanie Hayden nodded. "Yeah. We asked. At Vinnie's. We thought you looked interesting. And someone said you play tennis. I've never picked up a racket in my life. Neither has Deacon. But we go to the matches. They're fun. Anyway, here you are, and here we are.

Not off to a very good start at Salem, are you?"

At first, Nicki thought Mel meant her lousy showing at practice that day. She quickly realized the girl was referring to her mishap on the highway. "That tire is brand-new," she said grimly.

Deacon bent to check it out. "Slashed," he said without hesitation. "Someone did a real number on this baby." He stood up. "Could be random. Or not." He looked down at Nicki, whose head came only to the collar of his black leather jacket. "Could somebody be this unhappy about your arrival in our hallowed, ivy-covered halls?"

Nicki was reminded of Libby's cold, green eyes. "Someone might be," she answered, "but how would they know this car was mine? There's nothing special about it. There must be dozens of light blue compact cars on campus."

"Not with a State sticker on the rear windows," Deacon said drily. "You might want to seriously consider removing that. On Salem's campus, that's like wearing a sign that says, 'Kick me.'"

Chagrined, Nicki nodded and said, "You're right. I forgot all about it. That's probably the reason for the tire, don't you think?"

"Seems a bit drastic to me," Deacon said,

"although I've noticed that a lot of people on campus use unfriendly terms when referring to State. Still, slashing a tire? I guess we won't know if the sticker is the reason unless you remove the sticker and nothing worse happens to you."

Nicki didn't like the sound of that. There might be more of this kind of thing?

The sticker wouldn't just peel off. She'd need hot water. "I'll do it first thing in the morning," she said.

"Maybe it wasn't the sticker at all," Mel suggested as they climbed into Deacon's sporty black car. "Maybe someone knew it was your car because they saw you getting in or out of it. I don't want to make you nervous or anything. I'm just saying, you might want to give some thought to who might want to make you miserable, that's all."

Nicki rode to town in the front seat between the two of them. The minute they were all seated, Deacon flicked a button and music filled the car at full volume. Conversation became impossible; Nicki was glad she didn't need to talk. She needed to calm down and think.

First, the mousse message on her locker door . . . a juvenile stunt, it seemed to her, something that kids in high school would do.

Not very original, even if they had used mousse instead of spray paint.

Ginnie had said it couldn't have been done by Libby DeVoe herself, but Pat had pointed out that Libby could have assigned the task to one of her many followers.

And now the tire. But Libby had only left her seat in Vinnie's once, as far as Nicki could remember, and then only to run to another table and gossip for a few minutes. She hadn't left the restaurant.

Besides, Libby seemed too obvious. She'd been so open about her feelings toward Nicki, she'd have to be crazy or stupid to try anything nasty so soon.

Maybe she *was* crazy. Nicki had read about dedicated athletes who became totally obsessed with their sport and stopped thinking rationally, often driving themselves to a point that endangered their physical and mental health.

Maybe that had happened to Libby DeVoe.

They stopped at the garage Mel had mentioned and were told someone would go get the car and have the tire changed within the hour.

"So," Deacon said as they left the garage, "where to now? What exactly was your destination when misfortune waylaid you?"

"The mall. I have to" . . . it sounded so silly

. . . "I have to exchange some socks."

"Socks." Deacon smiled at her. "Ah, yes, those little white things you wear under your sneakers when you wow them on the courts. Very important, those little white socks. We shall take you to the mall and you shall have footwear. This is the least we can do for good old Salem U."

He didn't talk like anyone else she knew. But she decided she liked it. Interesting. Deacon Skye was interesting, and the fact that he didn't play tennis, never had, intrigued her even more. She had, in the past, dated boys who didn't play tennis. But because they knew she did, they had talked about it at length. She had hated that. There was more to her than tennis. A lot more.

Deacon had a different look, too, although she couldn't really put her finger on what it was. It wasn't just the black jacket, jeans, and boots. His features were sharp and, she suspected, could probably look cruel. Long, straight nose, dark eyebrows, and intelligent eyes that looked almost black. Not Mel Gibson, though. More like Christian Slater. She was positive those eyes never missed a thing, and wondered if anyone had ever tried to hide anything from him. If they had, they'd probably failed.

When the three walked into the sporting goods shop, John Silver, back at work and waiting on a customer, gave Nicki an inquisitive look. Two minutes later, he was at her side, as Deacon and Mel stopped to carry on a perfectly serious conversation with a male mannequin dressed in ski wear.

"What are you doing with them?" John asked. "They don't play tennis."

To a non-tennis player, it might have seemed like an odd comment, but Nicki knew exactly what he meant. We all stick together, she told herself. But that's probably a mistake, because then we never meet anyone interesting, like Deacon, and Mel.

"Do you know them?" she asked John, handing him the package of socks she wanted exchanged.

"Everyone knows them," he said with a tolerant smile. "They're always in trouble."

"Murder and mayhem?" she asked lightly, smiling at him.

He laughed. "No, nothing that dramatic. They're just . . . well, they like breaking the rules, that's all. I wouldn't think you would have anything in common with those two."

Exactly what she'd thought at Vinnie's. "I was stranded on the highway, and they gave me a ride, that's all." And they were nicer to me than most of the tennis team, she thought.

"No qualms about getting into a car with them?" he asked as she searched the racks for exactly the right kind of sock. "I'm not sure I'd do it."

"You didn't have to. Nobody slashed your tire."

He was clearly shocked. "Your tire was slashed? Are you sure?"

"Oh, I'm sure, all right. And judging by the reception I got at practice today, it could very well have been done by one of my oh-so-friendly teammates." The thought stunned her. She hadn't been aware that she'd been thinking such a thing, except for Libby, of course.

John nodded at that. "They didn't make you feel welcome? That was Libby's doing, I'll bet. I told you to watch out for her."

"I know you did. She's really something. Great player, though."

John shook his head. "Tire-slashing doesn't seem like Libby's thing. But I guess you never know, do you? I repeat my earlier advice, Nicki. Watch your back. And," nodding toward Deacon and Mel, who had taken up positions in an inflated rubber raft on the floor and were pretending to row, John added, "you might want to give a little more thought to who you choose to hang with at Salem. Maybe you should pick people you have more in common with than Bonnie and Clyde over there."

"You mean, I should stick to tennis players like myself," Nicki said with an impish grin. "Well, to tell you the truth, John, I'm a little sick of conversations revolving around serves and backhands. I might even take up a new sport. Something like, oh, say, river rafting." And taking the package John handed her, she strode purposely over to the rubber raft and climbed in to sit beside Mel, who handed her an oar.

Deacon broke into a chorus of "Row, Row, Row, Your Boat," and Mel and Nicki joined in.

John watched for a while and then, shaking his head, left to search the storeroom for a pair of size thirteen Nikes needed by a customer.

Nicki was having so much fun, she didn't even notice that he'd gone.

Chapter 5

When they left the sporting-goods store, Deacon led them to a bookstore. "His father writes travel books," Mel told Nicki as they walked. "Every time we come here, we go into the bookstore and turn all of his father's books face front so they'll sell better. It's fun."

"Your father travels a lot?" Nicki asked Deacon.

"Not just my father. We all did. When he went, we went, too, all six of us. My dad has itchy feet. Can't stand to live in one place for more than a year. I went to twelve schools in twelve years."

"That beats my record," Nicki said drily. He was the first person she'd ever met who had the same background she did. So they did have something in common.

"Don't tell me your father writes travel books, too," Mel said with a grin.

"No. Military. Eight schools in twelve years. I hated it."

"Yeah?" Deacon looked surprised. "Man, I loved it. By the time I was ten, I couldn't wait for the next place. I'm going into civil engineering, building bridges, that kind of stuff, so I can move around all the time and get paid for it."

Nicki decided they didn't have that much in common, after all. When she had her own place, she was going to stay there forever. She'd had enough of moving.

"The thing about moving," Deacon said then, "is, no one ever finds out who you really are, and you leave your mistakes behind. You don't have to live with them."

Startled, Nicki glanced over at him. What a weird thing to say. Why would it be a good thing that no one ever found out who you really were? That was one of the things she'd hated about moving. Never really getting to know people. Deacon sounded like he had found that a positive thing. But if you were always running away from your mistakes, when did you learn not to make the same ones?

Well, whatever Deacon Skye's mistakes were, it wasn't any of her business how he handled them.

When they had finished putting Arthur

Skye's travel books face forward, they left the bookstore for the food court where they talked about moving while they ate, and where Mel went into the smoking section to collect all of the ashtrays and toss them into a trash container. "I'm saving lives," she responded calmly when Nicki pointed out that the mall management had paid for those ashtrays.

When they had eaten, Deacon moved to the piano sitting just inside the entrance and pounded out two rock melodies before a security officer came along and told him to "Beat it, kid. You want to play piano here, you go to the mall employment office and fill out an application."

The security officer followed them as they left the food court and window-shopped their way out of the mall. It seemed to Nicki that Deacon deliberately walked very slowly, pausing to scrutinize every single window as they passed each shop, his voice unnaturally loud as he made critical comments about the displayed merchandise.

Deacon is daring that officer to throw us out of here, she realized. Maybe getting tossed out of malls was one of the "mistakes" Deacon had referred to earlier.

Nicki breathed a sigh of relief when they finally arrived at the main entance. Watching them warily, the security guard didn't turn away until they had actually gone through the glass double doors and were standing outside.

They were almost to the parking lot when Mel pulled a keychain from her pocket and held it up in the air. "Cute, isn't it?" she said triumphantly. "I love the little teddy bear."

"I didn't see you buying anything," Nicki said, puzzled.

"Buying?" Mel laughed. "I didn't *buy* it, Nicki. It was hanging right there on the counter on a little rack in the bookstore, just begging to be given a good home. So I obliged."

"You stole it?"

"Oh, 'stole' is such a harsh word. This little teddy bear was lonesome. I took pity on him, that's all. He'll be much happier with me than he was hanging on that rack."

Nicki waited for Deacon to say something. But he remained silent, striding along nonchalantly as if the conversation between the two girls had nothing to do with him.

"Geez, Nicki," Mel said, laughing, "we're talking less than two bucks here. Chill out. You think the store is going to go broke over two bucks?"

"Forget it," Nicki said brusquely. She wasn't about to deliver a lecture on honesty to someone she hardly knew. But she found herself increasingly uncomfortable with the pair. Maybe John Silver had been right. If she got into any trouble with these two, her scholarship would be in jeopardy. "If you'll just take me back to the garage now, I'm sure my car is ready."

As they reached Deacon's car, Nicki felt his eyes on her. For one nervous moment, she thought he was going to refuse to take her back to the garage; thought that he had sensed her disapproval of Mel's stunt, and was going to leave her stranded in the mall parking lot late at night.

But he merely shrugged and said, "Sure. No problem."

During the drive to the garage, Mel hummed to herself and swung the keychain in the air, as if she were deliberately taunting Nicki with it.

The car wasn't quite ready, but Nicki insisted Deacon and Mel go on to school without her. "It'll be done soon," she told them, gazing up at her car suspended on a rack, instead of looking at Deacon. "I don't mind waiting. Thanks for the ride."

"Any time. See you around." Something about his tone of voice told Nicki he didn't really expect to see her around. He thinks I'm a drag, she thought, and couldn't be sure if that was annoying, because she didn't think of herself that way, or disappointing, because she didn't want *him* to think of her that way.

Smiling, keychain in hand, Mel waved out the window as they pulled away.

When her car was finally ready, Nicki drove back to campus in a mood that matched the night's darkness. If she had hit it off with Deacon and Mel, it wouldn't have mattered as much that the tennis team, for the most part, hadn't welcomed her with open arms. Now, all she had to look forward to was going back to her empty, lonely little room.

She should have stayed at State. At least there, she'd had friends. No one there had snubbed her or left nasty messages on her locker or slashed her tires.

But State had only offered her a partial scholarship.

To her complete astonishment, Deacon was waiting at her door when she arrived. Black baseball cap pulled down over his eyes, he was leaning against the wall, hands in the pockets of his black jeans.

"What are you doing here?" she asked bluntly, reaching for her room key. More surprising than the sight of him was the fact that she was glad to see him.

He pushed the cap backward and stood up

straight. "Meaning, the last person in the world you expected to see waiting for you was me. Is there someone else you'd rather have standing sentinel at your door?"

She shook her head no.

He nodded. "Good. I just thought you might like to know that Mel likes to give the impression that she's a rebel, but the fact is, she's an amateur. The most rebellious thing she's ever done is probably palming that key chain. She was showing off. For you. I saw the look on your face. I decided to set the record straight."

"Well, it's not like I thought she was a hardened criminal," Nicki said, opening her door.

Deacon laughed. "A hardened criminal to you is probably someone who's never played tennis, am I right? And by the way, Mel was wrong about me. She said I'd never picked up a racket. Actually, I did play once, when I was too young to know better. Liked the game. Disliked intensely the people who played it."

Nicki felt her cheeks flushing. "Everyone? How can you lump together in one big bunch everyone who's ever played tennis?"

He shrugged. "I played at a country club. Everyone there was filthy rich. Even though I liked the game, I wasn't about to spend time with a bunch of spoiled brats."

"I play," Nicki said. "And I'm not rich." If

I were, she thought to herself, I could have stayed at State. And I would have.

"So I was wrong. Not for the first time, nor the last. Are we square about Mel's temporarily sticky fingers? You willing to give us another chance if I promise we won't all end up in the penitentiary?"

Nicki laughed. "Well, you'll have to promise, because I already moved once this year and I'm not going to pack my bags again any time soon."

He gave her a mock salute. "You have my word on it. Invite me in and we'll seal the deal."

"No, I . . ." She had moved through the doorway and would have turned then to tell him no, she wasn't inviting him in, she was too tired, but something stopped her.

What stopped her was the sight of her beloved tennis racket, hanging by a string from the light fixture in the center of the ceiling.

By a string . . .

There shouldn't have *been* a string. The racket that she had lovingly packed away in its case, which she had then zipped and stashed under her bed as she always did, had had no loose strings with which to hang it from the ceiling. A racket with a broken string was of no use at all to a tennis player.

But that one string, tied around the fiberglass handle, wasn't the worst part.

"Oh, no," Nicki breathed, and Deacon, hearing her, moved to stand behind her, gazing into the room.

The tennis racket which Nicki's father had given her in her sophomore year, the racket that felt like a part of her and had led her to victory in countless matches, was completely ruined. Every single string had been sliced through.

Chapter 6

"Looks like it went through a shredder," Deacon said, walking over to stare up at the suspended racket. The broken strings flopped uselessly as the racket dangled above the floor, like a sick decoration.

When the ugly sight had finally registered completely, Nicki began to tremble with rage. What a horrible thing to do!

Reaching up, Deacon released the racket. Instead of handing it to Nicki, he held it in his hands, turning it over several times, fingering the shredded string ends. "Not easy to cut," he remarked. "I wonder what they used."

What difference does it make? Nicki thought as she fought tears of anguish. "I don't know," she said aloud, "I don't know what they used. And I don't know how they got into my room, either."

"Are you kidding?" Deacon handed her the

useless racket. "The locks on these doors wouldn't keep a flea out if it wanted in. Locking them is a waste of time."

But Nicki wasn't listening. The minute Deacon placed the racket in her hands, her eyes widened. She studied the handle carefully. Same brand, same style, same color . . . but there was something . . . something not quite . . .

She hefted the racket, took a few practice swings, aware that the shredded strings would create a difference in feel. She knew that. But there was something about the way the racket felt in her hands that aroused hope in her. It *looked* exactly like her racket. But something felt wrong, something more than simply the shredded strings.

"Wait a sec," she said, and handed the damaged racket back to Deacon. She hurried over to her bed, got down on her knees, and reaching under the hem of the scarlet bedspread, withdrew the red plastic zippered case.

The case wasn't unzipped. And . . . it wasn't empty, as it should have been if that was really her racket in Deacon's hands. Her fingers shook as she yanked at the zipper. Then her fingers closed around the pale blue fiberglass handle inside. She pulled it forward.

And there it was. Her racket. Her very own

special racket that her father had given her. Completely intact. Every crisscrossed string whole, perfectly in place, and drawn taut.

Weak with relief, she sank back on her haunches, the racket clutched in her hands. "This," she said, "is my racket. That one," pointing to the butchered instrument in Deacon's hands, "isn't."

Still holding the wreckage in his hands, Deacon sat down in Nicki's desk chair. "Explain," he said. "I'm confused. This isn't yours?"

"No." She held high the one in her hands. "This is mine. I don't know who that one you're holding belongs to, or why it was chopped to pieces, but it isn't mine, and that's all I care about."

"It shouldn't be." Deacon was frowning at her.

"What?"

"That your racket is still in one piece shouldn't be all you care about. You should care that your room was invaded. You should care that a racket exactly like yours was butchered and then hung from your ceiling light. And above all, you should care that someone went to a lot of trouble to make you think they'd destroyed something you care a lot about."

Nicki thought about that. She knew he was right. Still, after the scare she'd just had, having her racket in her hands, safe and sound and intact, made it hard to focus on the things Deacon had mentioned.

"Maybe," she said slowly, getting up to sit on her bed, "the tennis team here has some kind of hazing ritual. You know, like fraternities and sororities sometimes have."

"That's not what this was, Nicki, and you know it," he persisted. "Hazing might involve hiding your racket, or painting it with glue or honey, or filling your ball can with trick balls. Juvenile, stupid things like that. But you're talking about people who love the game themselves. They wouldn't deliberately destroy another player's racket as a joke. Or even pretend to."

Again, Nicki knew he was right.

"You should call security. Or at least your RA," he said, standing up. "And ask for a better lock on your door."

"I will," she promised, trying to think clearly. It wasn't a joke? A prank? It wasn't some silly kind of initiation rite for the new arrival? Then what *was* it? "And thanks for . . . for being here, Deacon."

"Want me to wait until the cavalry arrives?" he asked, hesitating near the door.

"No." She wanted to be alone, to think. "I'll call someone, I promise." She meant it. The idea that someone could get into her room without leaving any evidence of a break-in made her blood run cold. Her little room was drab and lonely, but it had never occurred to her that it might be unsafe.

"Look," he said, opening the door, "do not let this rattle you, okay? I know I said you should take it seriously, but maybe you were right. Maybe it was just a pathetic attempt at humor. The tennis players I knew when I was a kid came up short in the humor department. Some of them might actually have thought this kind of thing was funny. Something about the hot sun beating down on their brains, I guess."

His words fell on deaf ears. Nicki was touched by his attempt to cheer her up, but she knew he'd been right in the first place. It hadn't been a joke.

When he'd gone, she called the Resident Advisor for her floor, a junior named Sela Templeton. Although Sela seemed to have a hard time understanding at first exactly what had happened, when she saw the damaged racket, she did call Security. The man, who clearly didn't understand at all, nevertheless promised to put a heftier lock on Nicki's door . . . the following day.

And how do I sleep tonight? she wondered fearfully.

"Maybe you should call a friend," Sela suggested. "Have them sleep over. I think you'd feel better."

Nicki wasn't about to admit that she didn't know anyone on campus well enough to invite them for a sleepover. "That's okay," she said, walking Sela to the door. "I'm so tired, I'll be asleep in five minutes."

But she wasn't. Although she was exhausted, she couldn't erase from her mind the image of the shredded racket dangling from her light fixture.

Deacon was right. It was a lousy trick to pull on a fellow tennis player, making them think that something as important as their racket had been destroyed. It was cruel. And she knew someone on the team had to have done it. Only another tennis player would understand just how cruel it really was.

Nicki's first reaction after she'd thought about it was that she didn't really want to play with people who could be so mean.

Then anger and indignation overcame fear and distress, and her second, firmer reaction was, I'm going to play the best tennis tomorrow at practice that I've ever played in my life. No one on that team is going to guess how rattled I was tonight. I'm going to blow their socks off tomorrow.

Her intention when she walked onto the tennis courts the next day was to prove that the stunt with the racket hadn't scared her off. To prove that Nicki Bledsoe didn't scare so easily. And to show whoever had wrecked that racket, broken into her room, and tied the unmistakable message to her light fixture, that she had no intention of cutting and running.

She had no way of knowing whether or not she'd achieved her goal. Only time would tell if the cruel prankster had given up. But what she did know, when practice was over and they all ran, sweaty and tired, to the locker rooms, was that she had impressed almost everyone on the team with her performance.

She started out slowly, off-balance because she knew that someone on the team was pulling some nasty pranks, and she had no way of knowing which player it was. But by concentrating with all of her might and keeping in mind every second the goal that she'd set for herself, she was soon playing against Barb with fierce zeal, serving up one ace after another and beating her with perfectly placed shots.

Her first realization that she was attracting

attention came during a brief break when she heard shouts of praise from onlookers sitting in the bleachers. She suddenly had her own little fan club. Then, as their calls of support reached the ears of her fellow players, she felt them watching her also.

And as she kept shooting the ball back across the net without missing a beat, slamming it back like a missile each and every time, her footwork dazzling, her concentration unbroken, the team members began applauding at the more remarkable shots.

Well! Nicki thought as she dove for a difficult return just inside the foul line, how *about* that! Eat dirt, Libby DeVoe.

She was exhausted, but triumphant, when the long practice match was over and she had won.

"Boy," Barb said as they walked off the court, "you take no prisoners, Nicki. You have not a shred of mercy anywhere in your bones." But she didn't sound angry, as Nicki was sure Libby would have.

John was there, too, beaming congratulations her way. "See?" he said, coming up to her to shake her hand. "I told you it would be better today. I'm always right about stuff like that."

Although her fellow players congratulated her on the way to the locker room, Nicki sensed reluctance on their part. They weren't, she realized, ready to embrace her with warmth and enthusiasm. That rankled. How many times was she going to have to prove herself? One more match like this one with Barb, and she'd be in bed for a week, recuperating. Every muscle in her body ached, and she knew from experience that the aching would intensify later. A hot tub was in order. The whirlpool at the infirmary was available for athletes. Maybe she'd try that.

When she entered the locker room, Libby, Nancy Drew, and Carla Sondberg were staring daggers in her direction. Nicki shrugged it off. She'd played well, and everyone knew it. So Libby didn't seem to matter very much at the moment.

"She knows you're a real threat now," Pat said, arriving at Nicki's side. "This is not good. Watch out for her."

"That's what John Silver said," Nicki replied, slipping her racket inside its case. "I didn't take him very seriously. Maybe I should have."

"Always take John seriously. He's a smart guy, and he knows what he's talking about. I think he has a thing for Ginnie."

"Ginnie? I thought all she cared about was tennis."

"True. I don't think she knows John is alive, even though he never misses a match. He knows Ginnie has only one love, and that's tennis, but I still think he's interested."

Coach Dietch emerged from her office to make an announcement. "Exhibition match, Sunday afternoon, here. I want to see how you all play in front of a crowd." Then she began rapidly rattling off play assignments.

Although Nicki was listening carefully, she heard only, "Bledsoe against DeVoe in singles play." Everything after that was blocked out, as if the shock had suddenly rendered her stone-deaf. She was playing Libby in front of a crowd? Great. Just great! As if things weren't sticky enough between them already.

If I lose, Nicki thought in dismay, Libby will be so smug and triumphant, she'll be even more unbearable than she is now. And if I, by some miracle, trounce her, well, a defeated Libby could be a dangerous thing.

Either way, *I* lose, Nicki told herself. She had never in her life deliberately played any less than her best. But the thought of how Libby might react to a public defeat by the "new girl" was so chilling, Nicki was momentarily tempted to develop a sudden, mysterious disease that would keep her off the courts on Sunday.

Because if Libby was the person already tormenting her, defeat at Nicki's hands would only make things worse.

And if she *wasn't* the one, if someone else had strung that racket from the ceiling, then defeating Libby in public would give Nicki *two* enemies to battle.

But the moment didn't last. No way was she going to hide out on Sunday. Deacon Skye might think that running away from things was a good answer, but Nicki Bledsoe didn't. Libby DeVoe wasn't scaring her off the courts.

Anyway, Nicki thought as she headed for the showers, maybe you won't beat her. She is very, very good. If she wins, if she hammers you into the ground in front of the whole school, you might be humiliated, but at least you won't have to look behind every bush after that to see if Libby is lurking behind it, waiting to get her revenge.

By the time she'd taken her shower, the only thing Nicki was sure of was that she was going to play on Sunday. And she was going to play her very best. Whatever came after that, she'd handle.

But her firm resolve did nothing to dissolve the hard lump of anxiety lying in her chest.

Chapter 7

"You're tying yourself up in knots over that exhibition match with DeVoe," Deacon said on Friday afternoon after classes. "What you need is to relax, have some fun, take the kinks out. How about we crash the Phi Delta Theta party tonight?"

Nicki had spent Wednesday and Thursday evenings with Deacon and Mel. She'd invited Pat and Ginnie to join them at the movies and later at Vinnie's on Thursday, but Pat said she was too broke for a movie and Ginnie said she was too tired.

Deacon and Mel were fun. Interesting. Different. There had been no more shoplifting, and they managed to make even the most ordinary excursion fun. And compared to most of the tennis team, the warmth they surrounded Nicki with was a welcome change.

Deacon and Nicki were sitting on the fountain wall on the Commons, a broad, level area green in spring and fall, but covered now with a thin layer of crusted old snow. The cloudy, cold, gray day suited Nicki's mood. Her spectacular performance at practice two days earlier had failed to thaw her teammates' resistance to her. And she hadn't repeated the performance since. On Thursday, she hadn't been assigned play at all and had spent the two hours practicing her backhand, and this afternoon, she'd played poorly, her nerves strung too tightly over the upcoming exhibition match. Barb and Hannah were still friendly, but no one else had thawed.

Thursday, when she'd found her sneakers knotted together after her shower, she had hoped that meant they were starting to include her. Later, the hairbrush she kept in her locker had been coated with peanut butter. That kind of stunt was supposed to mean you were being welcomed to the team. But since there was no other sign that that was true, Nicki suspected that Ginnie or Patrice, maybe both of them, were pulling the stunts, trying to make her feel at home.

It wasn't working. Nicki felt like a foreign exchange student who didn't speak the language. She had never felt this alienated anywhere.

Deacon was right. She needed a party, even if she had to crash one.

"Sure," she said, "a party sounds great."

But it wasn't.

It started out okay. No one raised an eyebrow when Deacon, dressed completely in black and Mel, wearing a tiny miniskirt, a khaki army shirt, and combat boots, walked into the Phi Delta Theta house with Nicki. No one asked who had invited them. Someone handed each of them a plastic cup filled with punch, and a boy from one of Mel's art classes came over and led her off to the dance floor. A number of people called out a greeting to Deacon, surprising Nicki. She hadn't known he had so many friends.

But just about the time when she thought they were actually going to have fun, a group of tennis players arrived, led by Libby DeVoe, who stopped short in the doorway when she saw Nicki.

"What are *you* doing here?" she said coldly, slipping out of her coat and revealing a flaming-red dress that, Nicki thought nastily, made her look like an oversized tube of lipstick. Glancing at Deacon, Libby added, "He's not a Phi Delt."

"Neither am I," Nicki answered cooly. "Couldn't pass the physical."

"Very funny. *Not*." Libby tossed her coat on

a chair. "What *are* you doing here? Shouldn't you be resting up for Sunday's match? Or in the gym working on your backhand? After the way you played yesterday, I'd think you'd want all the practice you could get."

Nicki nonchalantly flicked an imaginary piece of lint from her blue velvet tunic. "Well, you'd be wrong, wouldn't you? But thanks for your concern, Libby. I can't tell you how much I appreciate it."

Barb and Hannah gave Nicki apologetic smiles. As Libby and her followers walked away, Nicki thought darkly, Which one of you broke into my room and tied that racket to my ceiling light? And what are you going to pull next?

Nancy Drew commented as she passed, "You shouldn't talk to Libby like that. No one else does."

"Oh, go solve a mystery!" Nicki turned to Deacon, saying, "Why don't we dance? I need to work off some of this frustration."

"Good idea," Deacon replied.

They danced four songs in a row, and then walked over to the refreshment table. Libby was standing off to one side, her narrowed green eyes shining like cold, hard jewels as she watched Deacon and Nicki.

"She hates me," Nicki said when Deacon

glanced Libby's way. "What did I ever do to her, anyway?"

"You showed up."

John came by then, and Deacon went off to locate Mel.

"You're a Phi Delt?" Nicki asked.

John smiled. He really was handsome. Ginnie had to be blind! "You sound surprised. You think only jocks are pledged to frats?"

Nicki flushed. "No, of course not. I didn't mean —"

"Lots of people do," he interrupted. "They think that if you're not a jock, you don't count. I used to think it myself, once upon a time, when I was young and stupid. Now, I know better. I love sports, but there are other important things in the world, too, Nicki."

"I know that," she said in a subdued voice. She hadn't meant to hurt his feelings. To change the subject, she said, "I almost had to come and see you this week." And she told him about the destroyed racket and how she had thought initially that it was her own. "Not that you could have restrung the thing," she concluded. "It was beyond hope."

John was still frowning. "Your kind of racket isn't that easy to shred," he said. "I wonder what was used on it?"

The same thing Deacon had said. Nicki

shrugged. "Who knows? A Cuisinart, maybe. Or a paper shredder." Then, out of simple curiosity, she asked, "How did you know what kind of racket I have? I haven't brought it into the shop yet."

He laughed. "I saw you practice the other day. I notice things like that.

"I hope you're not letting Libby get to you." He smiled down at her. "I've seen that girl throw her racket all the way across a court. More than once. I'd play it cool around her."

"I will, I promise. Thanks." To repay him for the advice, she said, "Ginnie didn't come tonight. She's home. You should have invited her."

This time, he was the one who looked surprised. His broad cheekbones flushed. "Me? How did you . . ."

"I'm smart, like you. Have you asked her out?"

"Nope. Because I *am* smart. She's already got a love. Tennis."

Well, at least she'd tried. A bunch of Phi Delts came over to talk to John then, and Nicki wandered off to find Deacon.

She found him in the kitchen with Mel. They were pouring the contents of two large bottles of tabasco sauce into a kettle on the stove.

"We're livening up this party," Mel explained. "It's much too quiet to suit me."

"What's in the kettle?"

"Sloppy joe mix." Mel gestured toward a huge platter piled high with hamburger buns, sliced open. "Whadya think?" she asked, smiling mischievously.

"I think you're going to get us kicked out of this party," Nicki said uneasily.

"And do you care?" Mel peered into Nicki's face. "Are you having fun yet?"

No, she wasn't, and no, she didn't care, Nicki realized. Too many tennis players giving her the cold shoulder, and always, always, there was Libby DeVoe, hate emanating from her pores like poisonous fumes.

"Why don't we just go?" she asked Deacon. "I'm ready if you are."

"Not. Just. Yet." He poured carefully, and when he had finished, took a fat wooden spoon from a rack over the stove, and stirred thoroughly. "The hordes will be hungry any minute now. Let's stay and watch the fun."

It *was* fun. Especially when Libby and Nancy Drew and the rest of Libby's crew piled sloppy joe high on their hamburger buns, oohing and aahing over how good the mixture looked and declaring that they were "starving." When they left the kitchen, plates in hand, Deacon, Mel, and Nicki followed silently, their faces devoid of expression. They took seats opposite the tennis crowd, and waited for the reaction.

It was worth the wait. Libby was the first to turn scarlet, choke, and gag before she jumped up and ran from the room. Nancy Drew was the second, and Carla Sondberg was right behind the two of them. Nicki did feel bad when Hannah and Barb raced out of the room as well, but she felt nothing but satisfaction when the remainder of Libby's group gasped, cried out, and ran to get water.

The trio was still laughing as they left the Phi Delta Theta house.

They were just about to climb into Deacon's car when John Silver came running out of the house, calling to them.

They stopped, waiting at the car for him.

"Don't you think you went a little overboard?" he asked quietly. "You ruined a perfectly good party."

Nicki was embarrassed. The prank suddenly didn't seem as funny as it had.

But Deacon said calmly, "I don't know what you're talking about."

"Oh, give me a break," John said. "Everyone knows you guys were responsible. You're the only ones who didn't run screaming and gasping into the kitchen for water. Besides, we all know that's exactly the kind of stunt you'd find hilarious." Looking directly at Nicki, he said, "Didn't I tell you? These two are going to make enemies for you, Nicki. And if there's one thing *you* don't need, it's more enemies." And with that, he turned and headed back into the house.

Chapter 8

Nicki spent all day Saturday practicing. She was up early, showered, dressed, and ready to go by eight o'clock. She hadn't slept well, and had a headache. But she was anxious to get out and make up for Wednesday's atrocious performance on the courts.

The atmosphere in the dome was even chillier than it had been. She knew everyone was remembering the previous night's culinary disaster. They all knew she'd been in on it, with Deacon and Mel. No one seemed the worse for wear, but they were clearly still angry.

"What's going on?" Pat asked Nicki when she noticed the ugly looks being directed Nicki's way as they were doing their warm-up exercises on the sidelines. And Ginnie said with concern, "Boy, if looks could kill!"

In a soft voice, Nicki told them the truth.

Pat didn't seem shocked. "Deacon's always

getting into trouble," she said matter-of-factly.

Ginnie wasn't quite so accepting. "John's right," she said, retying her sneaker laces. "You probably shouldn't be hanging around with those two. If Coach hears about your pranks, you could get into trouble."

"What I do off the courts," Nicki said stiffly, "is my own business. And Deacon and Mel are fun. They're not snobs, like some other people I could mention."

Now, Pat looked shocked. "You don't mean us, do you?"

"Of course not. But you two are just about the only people on this team who've spoken to me." Nicki shook her head. "And I don't get it. I just don't get it. It can't be just Libby. How can one person have that much power over other people?"

"Maybe it isn't just her," Pat suggested, opening a new tin of tennis balls. "She isn't the only one on the team worried that you're going to take her place. There are others."

But before Nicki could ask who those "others" were, Coach blew the whistle signifying the official beginning of practice, ending the conversation.

In spite of the butterflies in her stomach, which seemed to be performing new gymnastic feats with every passing moment, Nicki played well. By noon, some of the players had thawed again, asking her how she achieved the control that she'd been displaying. As gratifying as that was, it failed to take the edge off her anxiety. The next day's exhibition loomed ahead of her. She could prepare for it by practicing, but she couldn't avoid it. There was nothing she could do to stop it.

She spent her lunch break with Pat and Ginnie, in Lester dorm's dining hall. Ginnie looked tired, and they still had an afternoon of practice to get through.

"Sometimes," Ginnie said wearily as they ate, "I think it might be nice to just hand everything over to Libby and go lie on a beach for a month."

"Bite your tongue," Nicki scolded. "Can you imagine what she'd be like if this team didn't have you? She'd really be top dog then. She'd probably hire a press agent, show up for practice in a limo, and expect an endorsement from an athletic shoe company."

"I know, but I get so tired. . . ." Ginnie's voice trailed off.

"We all do," Pat said sharply, surprising Nicki. "But stop being a wimp." In a milder voice, she added, "Quit whining, and eat. Your problem is, you never let go. We should have gone to the Phi Delta Theta party last night."

She grinned at Nicki, but her voice was a little envious. "It sounds like it might have been fun. And the food was free."

Nicki laughed. "But inedible. Still, you both should have come." To Ginnie, she said casually, "John was there. He hasn't called you, has he?"

"I turned the phone off at nine. Went to bed. I was so tired." Ginnie lifted her head. "Why would John be calling me? What for?"

"Give me a break," Pat said drily. "What *for*? Well, you're a girl, and he's a guy, and . . ."

At first, Ginnie looked pleased. Then the expression disappeared, and she said quickly, "Oh, I don't have time for that stuff now. Not with this marathon practice today and the exhibition tomorrow. John knows how tough it is. He knows I'm too tired to go out at night."

She sounded so disapproving, Nicki felt her cheeks flush. Was Ginnie implying that Nicki wasn't as dedicated as she should be? Because she'd been having fun with Deacon and Mel? "There's more to life than batting a little round ball back and forth across a net," she said, getting up and collecting her trash.

Ginnie looked up in surprise. "No, there isn't," she said quietly. "Not for me."

Nicki felt a sudden, sharp pang of pity. She

loved tennis, too. But she also liked music, and dancing, and reading, and roller-skating, and movies. If something ever happened that kept her from playing tennis again, it wouldn't be the end of the world.

But for Ginnie it would.

"Time to practice," Nicki said aloud, jumping up. Pat groaned. But not Ginnie. She led the way back to the courts.

Nicki played as well during the afternoon hours as she had that morning, but, by the end of the practice session, every muscle in her body was screaming for respite. "I don't know about anyone else," she said as they all dragged into the locker room, "but I'm hitting the whirlpool at the infirmary. Because if I don't, I will have to be carried onto the courts tomorrow afternoon."

Everyone else had plans. Of course they do, Nicki reflected bitterly, heading across the cold, twilighted campus for the infirmary. Anyone who's anyone has plans on Saturday night.

Not that she hadn't had the opportunity. Deacon had planned to take her dancing in town. She'd turned him down, knowing she'd be too tired. He hadn't been happy about it, but he'd said he understood. She hoped he meant it.

She was almost to the infirmary when she

heard a voice behind her, calling her name. She turned to find Barb hurrying along the walkway toward her, her tall, bony figure shadowy in the twilight of campus.

"Changed my mind," she said breathlessly. "My muscles were shrieking at me, 'Whirlpool, whirlpool!' I decided to give them a break. Okay if I join you?"

Nicki was glad to have the company, and even happier when they entered the infirmary and discovered that there were no patients at all and only a nurse on duty. She was half-asleep, sitting with her feet up on the desk, listening to music.

Nicki knew that being in the almost-deserted building by herself would have been too creepy.

The whirlpool room was deserted, too, the small, square, windowless space dark, the water in the octagonal, tile-edged tub at peace.

"I'll start it up while you change," Nicki offered. "Let's not turn the lights on. It'll be more peaceful in the dark." She flipped a switch on the tub, and the water began churning vigorously, making gurgling noises. "Do I need this! The aches in my muscles have aches." Stripping down to her bodysuit and wrapping a clean towel around her hair, she climbed into the tub and sank to a sitting position. The warm, bubbling water wrapped around her like a heated cocoon. It felt delicious.

"This is perfect," Barb said when she got in and relaxed against the back of the tub. "Absolutely perfect. And you were right about the lights. It's much better in the dark. Like swimming in warm, tropical waters under a night sky."

Nicki laughed. "Like that's something you've done recently?"

"It's something I've *never* done, but I can use my imagination, can't I? And you didn't need to put a towel over your hair. My hairdryer is right there on the chair. You're welcome to use it."

"You put an electrical appliance this close to the tub?" Nicki demanded. "Are you nuts? What if it falls into the water? We'll fry! Then we won't have to worry about any stupid exhibition."

"It's not plugged in, silly girl. I'm not that dumb," Barb assured her.

"Thanks for the offer," Nicki said, "but I brought my own hairdryer. But maybe I should just forget about it, and brave the elements with soaking wet hair. If I got pneumonia, I wouldn't have to go up against DeVoe tomorrow."

"Don't sweat it. You're ready for DeVoe. I

was watching you at practice today. Very impressive. Quit worrying. Wish I were in your league, but I'm not." Barb smiled lazily, her eyes closed, her cheeks rosy from the humidity. "One of the advantages to not being one of the best is, it's not the end of the world when you lose, because you've lost before, and will again."

"You're a good tennis player, Barb."

"Yeah, I know. *Good* is enough for me. It wouldn't be for Libby, though. Ginnie, either. Maybe not even for you."

They fell silent then, luxuriating in the warm, bubbling water, and Nicki thought about Barb's remark. Would she have been satisfied to be just "good" at tennis? It wasn't as if her parents had pushed her. Nicki had worked so hard at conquering tennis because she had to use it to gain entry into each new school she attended. No one would have paid much attention to someone who was only "good" at tennis. She had to be better than that. And so she had been.

But if it ended now, if Libby creamed her tomorrow, if the team refused to accept her totally, if Coach should shake her head sadly and say, "I'm terribly sorry, Nicole, but you just aren't as good as I thought you were," would it wreck her life?

No. It might Ginnie's, and it certainly would Libby's, but not Nicki Bledsoe's.

That realization momentarily stilled the butterflies in her stomach. She would play her very best tomorrow. But if Libby beat her, she'd still survive.

"This is not perfection, after all," Barb said, sitting up. "Something is missing. Music, that's what's missing. That nurse at the desk has a tape player. I saw it. Maybe she'll let us borrow it for a few minutes. We can plug it in right over there."

Nicki sat up, too. The water was making her too sleepy. "Good idea. I'll go get it. If I don't, I'm going to sack out in this water, and that wouldn't be good." She climbed out of the whirlpool, and wrapped a towel around herself. Then she ran in her bare feet, dripping all the way, to the door. "Don't go away, I'll be right back."

"You're going to leave me here in the dark all alone?" Barb called, faking alarm.

"You're not alone. You have all those bubbles. Relax."

Nicki made the long trek to the nurse's desk to find her on the telephone. Nicki stood off to one side, waiting impatiently. She was shivering with cold, her arms wrapped around her chest and aware that she was creating a very large puddle on the white tile at her feet. Since the nurse was laughing, it was clear that her conversation had nothing to do with a medical emergency.

Finally, when she couldn't stand the cold another second, Nicki moved forward to the desk to say, "Excuse me?"

The nurse looked up, annoyed. "Yes?"

"We're using the whirlpool and we were wondering if we could borrow your tape player? Just for a few minutes? I mean, since you're on the telephone . . ."

The nurse shrugged and reached behind her to unplug the black, oblong radio/recorder. "Don't drop it in the whirlpool," she said, holding one hand over the mouthpiece. "Not only would you get electrocuted, which would be very messy for me, but you'll ruin that tape, and it's one of my favorites. Vince Gill. Don't you just love country?'

Well, no, Nicki didn't, but even country was better than nothing.

Slipping and sliding, she tried to hurry back to the whirlpool room, anxious to be enveloped in that warm, silky water again.

"Country!" she announced drily as she pulled the door open with her free hand and stepped into the dark, quiet room. "The nurse is into country music. But it *is* music, right? Now, we can *really* relax." Closing the door behind her, she advanced toward the whirlpool, aiming for the electrical outlet where she intended to plug in the tape player.

No response from Barb probably meant that she'd fallen asleep. Nicki had almost dozed off earlier herself. The water was so warm, so soothing, and they were both so tired. But she'd have to wake Barb up. Taking a nap in a whirlpool wasn't healthy. Bad for the blood pressure or something.

"Barb?" she queried as she crouched to feel around with one hand for the outlet. "Wake up! I'm going to have to turn the light on to find a place for this plug."

No answer.

"Barb?" Nicki's searching fingers found the plastic outlet cover. But they touched something else as well. Something that shouldn't have been there.

A plug. There had been no plug in that outlet when she left the whirlpool room. She knew because she'd checked, intending to use it for her hairdryer when they got out of the water. There had been, as in all outlets, two receptacles for plugs. Both had been empty. Two empty slits on top, two on the bottom, waiting for the prongs of an electrical cord to be inserted.

But now there *was* a cord there.

Nicki's heart began to pound painfully. "Barb?" Nicki stood up and moved closer to the whirlpool.

She couldn't see clearly enough to be certain the plug belonged to the hairdryer, but she knew in her heart that it did. Knew it with nauseating certainty.

The hairdryer that they'd been so careful with, for safety's sake, wasn't safe now. Not safe at all. It was firmly connected to a source of powerful, deadly electricity.

And just then, a harsh, husky, unidentifiable voice came at Nicki out of the darkness. "Why did you leave the lights off?" the voice accused angrily over the bubbling of the whirlpool. "I couldn't *see* in the dark. She was *supposed* to be you. I *thought* she was *you*! This is *your* fault."

Hands grasped Nicki and shoved her toward the whirlpool.

Chapter 9

Nicki screamed.

For one awful moment she danced a deadly dance with the shadow of death. Then she heard the sound of footsteps in the hall. Heard the nurse calling, "What is it? What's wrong?"

The shadowy figure hissed, turned, and ran out of a side door.

Nicki fell to the floor on her stomach, one arm still outstretched, head lifted, eyes on the whirlpool. She couldn't scream, couldn't cry out, her voice completely paralyzed by what she had seen. It couldn't have happened. It couldn't have. No. *No!*

The words "She was supposed to be *you*" rang in her head.

"What happened to the lights?" the nurse cried in an annoyed voice as she burst into the room. She flipped on the light switch.

Nicki, heard the nurse cry out, "Oh, no, oh,

good Lord, no!", heard her soft, white-shod footsteps rushing to the supply closet in the corner where she grabbed a mop and used the wooden handle to knock the plug free of the outlet. Then Nicki heard swishing, splashing sounds as the nurse hauled Barb's lifeless body out of the water and laid her on the floor.

"I *told* you, I told you," the nurse muttered frantically as she bent to begin CPR on Barb, "I warned you about that radio . . ."

Nicki pulled herself to a sitting position. "It wasn't the radio," she said numbly, uselessly. "It wasn't the radio."

Everything became very confused then. The nurse, finding CPR futile, shouted to Nicki to call for help. But finding Nicki too upset to move, the nurse raced to a telephone, made some calls, ran back to Barb, began working on her again. Nicki sat on the floor watching with dull eyes.

"She was *supposed* to be *you* . . ."

Then other people came, Barb was taken away on a stretcher, and people in uniforms, police, Nicki thought, although she wasn't sure of anything, began asking her questions. Speaking in a monotone, she answered their questions. It wasn't the radio, she said. It was the hairdryer, she said. She said there was someone in the whirlpool room, and he had said

Barb was supposed to be her. . . .

She could hear a voice rambling on and on in that weird, deadened monotone and she wondered who it was that was talking so much in a dead voice. It couldn't be Barb. Barb couldn't talk. Barb was dead. Dead.

No, no . . .

After a while, the nurse asked who could she call to come and get Nicki, and it took Nicki a long time to think of Pat's name.

But she must have, because after another long while, Pat and Ginnie appeared in the doorway, tears of shock and horror on their faces, and took a speechless, shivering Nicki back to the dorm.

Ginnie kept saying in an awed voice, "I can't believe it. I can't believe it."

They put Nicki to bed and slept on the floor of her room, with a chair propped up underneath the doorknob. They asked her no questions. Pat put an extra blanket on her because she couldn't stop shaking, and Ginnie brought her a glass of water, which Nicki couldn't drink.

Nicki lay in bed with her eyes wide open, staring at nothing, long after the other two girls had fallen asleep.

He was looking for *you*, her mind told her. Barb was supposed to be you.

He'd be mad now. Madder than before. Because he hadn't done what he'd set out to do. Kill Nicole Bledsoe.

Why, why, *why*?

What had she done to make someone want to kill her?

"Aren't you the one who had that racket dangling from her ceiling?" the security guard who had accompanied the Twin Falls police had asked her at the infirmary.

Nicky had barely managed a nod.

"Someone have it in for you?" he'd asked, taking out a small notepad and a pen. "You got a feud going with someone on campus?"

A feud? Nicki tried to think. No, she wasn't engaged in a feud. Except for Libby. And she didn't *hate* Libby.

Besides, Libby wouldn't do something like this.

Would she?

When she had convinced the police that she had no idea who had dropped the hairdryer into the whirlpool, they gave up, saying they'd let her know what their investigation showed. They seemed so sure they'd learn all of the answers to all of her questions.

As if that would bring Barb back.

The infirmary, she thought, rolling over on her side and closing her eyes, was supposed to be where you went to get *well*. It was supposed to be a safe place. But it hadn't been for Barb.

If the infirmary wasn't safe, what *was?*

Nicki had no idea.

She stayed in bed for four days. Police officers came and went, Deacon and Mel showed up every day, Pat and Ginnie constantly came to the room to check on her, telling her that all of campus was stunned.

Nicki stayed in bed. She was waiting . . . waiting for a policeman to come and tell her they had arrested the madman who had killed Barb and that it was now safe to leave her room again.

But they didn't come.

On the fourth day, Coach called.

"We need you, Nicki. I understand that you've had a terrible shock. We all have. But staying in your room won't make it go away. The best thing to do is deal with it, and the best way to do that is to go on with your own life. I don't mean to sound hard-hearted. But you're not doing Barb any good by staying in bed. I postponed the exhibition matches for one week. Can I expect you at practice this afternoon?"

If I go out there, Nicki thought, staring down at the telephone in her hand, I'll be killed. Like Barb. Because he was looking for *me.*

But Coach was right. She couldn't stay in

her room forever. Life went on . . . for everyone except Barb Skinner.

"Yes," she said mechanically, "I'll be there."

The atmosphere in the locker room later that day was nightmarish. People were snapping at each other, faces were grim, arms and legs moved sluggishly, in slow motion, as if they were weighted down.

Nicki sat on a bench, staring at the floor. She didn't speak to anyone.

But at least she was there.

When she returned to her room after practice, Deacon and Mel were sitting on the floor in the hall. They stood up when she approached. "Where have you been?" Mel asked irritably. "I can't believe you went to practice, after what happened. Hasn't it occurred to you that the person with the hairdryer was probably a jealous tennis player? That was the first thing we thought of."

Nicki shrugged. "You *don't* know it was a tennis player. It could have been anyone." Now, she was sorry she'd told them what Barb's killer had said about finding the wrong person in the whirlpool. Of course they had jumped to the conclusion that it was someone on the team. She shouldn't have said anything. "Look, I'm really tired," she said, opening the door. "I'll talk to you tomorrow, okay?"

Mel looked disappointed. She tossed her long, wavy hair and her lower lip jutted forth. "Oh, Nicki, you're not going to go into hiding again, are you? I know it's been a terrible week for you, but you need to get out and have some fun."

Why did people insist on telling her what she should do? "Not tonight. I can't." Nicki leaned against the wall. "My legs feel like Jell-O. I'm beat. Coach has decided to go ahead with the exhibition, so I've got a week of practice ahead of me. Sorry."

"If I'd got to the locker room sooner the other night," Deacon said, "you'd never have gone to that whirlpool. I was coming to take you out to eat, but when I got there, Pat said you'd already gone to the whirlpool."

"Not your fault," Nicki said. "Forget it." If they didn't leave in the next sixty seconds, she was going to fall asleep leaning against the door. "It's not your job to protect me, Deacon. You're not my bodyguard."

"Well, maybe you need one."

Maybe she did.

"We'll be there Sunday," Mel said. "We wouldn't miss it."

Deacon nodded. "And we will make our presence *known!* That's a promise."

"Deacon," Nicki warned, "please don't get

yourself thrown out, okay? I need all the support I can get, especially right now. Without you two there, who would cheer for me?" Besides, she'd feel safer knowing Deacon and Mel were among the spectators.

"John," Mel said. "John Silver. He'll be there. And he likes you, I can tell. He'll be rooting for you."

"Not after that sloppy joe fiasco," Nicki reminded her.

Mel shrugged. "John doesn't hold a grudge. I do, but not him." She peered closely at Nicki. "You like him, don't you?"

"I guess so. What's not to like?"

"And even if he is still mad," Mel added as they reached the elevator, "he can't stand Libby DeVoe, so he'll be rooting for you, no matter what."

"Well, please don't get yourselves tossed out of the dome," Nicki said firmly. "It's bad enough that I have to practice and play when all I really feel like doing is sleeping. If I have to do this, I want my friends there."

Deacon saluted as Nicki began to close the door. "Yes, ma'am. Whatever you say, ma'am. We promise." Then he smiled at her, his dark eyes warm. "Get a good night's sleep."

He didn't say how she was supposed to do that when she kept seeing Barb, floating lifelessly in the whirlpool, her eyes staring emptily at the ceiling . . .

That hairdryer had been meant for *her*. If she'd been in the whirlpool alone, as she'd originally thought she would be, and the intruder had come in, she would be dead now.

Don't think ifs, she told herself sternly. Ifs are nothing but trouble. Reality is bad enough, all by itself.

Using the fierce concentration that she'd learned on the tennis courts, Nicki was finally able to shut out all the terrifying ifs and sleep.

But sometime later, she jerked upright, crying out.

"I threw the racket," she said into her empty room, her voice dazed. "I threw it. I shouldn't have. I didn't mean to. I was sorry right away, but it was too late. It was my fault."

Her eyes flew open, but they were glazed with sleep. "I didn't mean it," she whispered, "I'm sorry. I'm so sorry."

And as she lay back down, some lucid part of her sleep-fogged brain knew she wasn't talking about Barb being mistaken for her in the whirlpool. She was talking about something else.

But she had no idea what that something was.

Chapter 10

Nicki remembered her nightmare when she awoke in the morning. In the dream, she had been sorry about something. Very sorry. She could still feel the terrible pang of regret that had stabbed her in the middle of the night, awakening her. But for what? She shook her head. Made herself let it go. After what had happened she was bound to have nighmares.

The week passed quickly. The police had found no clues, no evidence leading to the identity of Barb's assailant. No fingerprints, no footprints, no one had seen anyone running from the infirmary. But they would keep investigating.

Lost in a fog of fear, Nicki went to classes and to practice, always with other people. The only time she spent alone was at the library, where she studied in the most secluded, shadowed corner she could find, trying to make herself invisible.

Deacon and Mel teased and cajoled, trying to talk her into "having some fun," but Nicki couldn't. She was safer in her room, with the new lock firmly fastened and her desk chair thrust underneath the doorknob.

"Nothing bad can happen when you're with us," Deacon argued.

But Nicki knew that wasn't true. Barb had been with someone when she died, hadn't she? And it hadn't done her any good at all.

The morning of the exhibition, Pat asked if Nicki was nervous about her match with Libby.

"No," Nicki lied. She'd always felt that if you admitted you were nervous before a match, if you gave voice to the thought, the thought became reality and spoiled your game. She wasn't willing to test that theory by telling the truth today. Besides, it wasn't really the match she was nervous about. It was being in the dome, out there on the open tennis courts without protection. Anyone could be among the spectators. *Anyone.*

There would be police there, she had been told. And university security guards. Everyone was looking for Barb's killer.

If only they'd found him before this exhibition.

Pat and Nicki donned sweats over their whites, Pat wishing aloud that she'd had the money for a new set, and left the room.

There didn't seem to be anything else Nicki could do about her fear except ignore it. That would be easier if she concentrated on something else. So she concentrated on her match with Libby.

Pat and Nicki joined John and Ginnie at their table for breakfast, and while they were eating, Deacon and Mel arrived. They seemed cool and standoffish to Nicki.

Still annoyed because I won't "go out and play" with them, she thought. Why couldn't they understand that it was all she could do right now to put one foot in front of the other?

No one talked about Barb. Nicki knew they all thought that would jinx the day. But their silence about the tragedy increased her feeling of disorientation. Barb had died, and here they all sat, eating and talking nervously about the exhibition, almost in the same way they would have if the horrible thing hadn't happened.

Scary.

The dome was already beginning to fill up when they went in to begin their warm-up. It was another cloudy, cold day, and those who would ordinarily have spent Sunday afternoon outside were opting for the warmth and comfort of the heated dome.

"It's going to be full," Pat observed as she and Nicki began lobbing balls back and forth. "The whole school will probably be here, so let's not fall flat on our faces. We'd never hear the end of it."

Libby arrived, walking into the dome as if, Nicki thought, it had been built especially for her. Carla and Nancy were right behind her, one carrying Libby's ball cans and fresh towels, the other Libby's rackets, still in their cases.

"That," Pat said drily, "is so Libby will have her hands free to wave to her adoring public. See?" Libby *was* waving to the spectators, with both hands. "She looks like one of those beauty queens riding in the back of a convertible in a parade, doesn't she?"

She did.

Nicki tried, and failed, to laugh. Barb should have been with Libby's entourage. But she wasn't. And never would be again.

Suddenly, Nicki wanted to beat Libby. More than anything. All of the confusion and terror and anger of the past week rose inside her and turned into a scalding anger against Libby. She had never wanted to beat anyone as intensely as she wanted to beat Libby. She didn't like the feeling, didn't like the anger brewing inside of her. It felt . . . dangerous, as if it might make her lose control. She couldn't win if she lost control.

But there it was, a fierce, urgent need to win, as if by doing so she could somehow erase the horror of the past week.

She tried reminding herself that it was the game, and the playing of it that mattered, not the opponent. Her father had taught her that.

But, glancing over at Libby, preening before the crowd, Nicki decided that even her father would make an exception in Libby's case. This time, it *was* the opponent that mattered.

Soon the matches began. Ginnie played first, against Nancy Drew.

"Ginnie's so sharp," Pat said as she and Nicki watched Ginnie's exhibition game battle from the sidelines. "She's fast, and she concentrates totally. *No* distractions — wish I could do that."

Although the match was exciting and resulted in a suspenseful tiebreaker, which Ginnie had to struggle to win, it was hard for Nicki to pay attention, knowing that she and Libby were up next.

I'm ready, she told herself firmly. Ready as I'll ever be.

She had scanned the stands a thousand times, looking for . . . what? For someone who looked as if he might be insane enough to electrocute someone in a whirlpool? What would that kind of person look like?

She had no idea.

She saw nothing out of the ordinary in the stands, although Deacon and Mel waved frantically every time she turned their way.

Students were acting as linesmen and referees, and John was going to act as ball person. A new can of balls was in place at his feet, under the bench.

"Relax," John cautioned as Nancy Drew went down to defeat and Nicki jumped to her feet.

"Easy for you to say," Nicki said drily. "I'd relax, too, if I could trade places with you."

As Libby ran out onto the court, waving at the crowd, her short, white skirt flying, Pat came up to Nicki and whispered, "You can take her. Forget about everything else, and relax, like John said. Staying cool is important."

"I know." Inhaling deeply and exhaling, Nicki took the balls that John handed her, clenched her racket handle, and strode out onto the court.

Libby sent her a sickeningly sweet smile from the opposite side of the net.

Right, Nicki thought grimly, and stretched up her arm to serve.

It was a grueling contest, the longest of the day. Libby DeVoe and Nicki Bledsoe were well-matched. Coach Dietch watched from the sidelines approvingly as the girls played their hearts out.

It seemed to Nicki that every time she pulled ahead, every time the pulse in her throat pounded, telling her that she might actually beat Libby, she double-faulted on her serve, or Libby sent a smashing return that no athlete in the world could have reached without breaking some bones. Time after time, Libby would assume a stance that should have meant a vigorous smash across the net. Time after time, Nicki would run to the back of the court to meet it, and would see a gentle lob that she had to race to the net to catch.

She became so lost in the match that she was scarcely aware of the spectators. She knew they were there, but they didn't matter. Only Libby mattered, only Libby's killer serve and murderous forehand.

Only winning mattered.

But every once in a while, when her concentration faltered momentarily, she would become aware of shouts from the sidelines. Those shouts, those voices, she knew, shouldn't have been breaking the silence during play. Tennis spectators were extraordinarily polite. They knew the rules. It wasn't like football, where people yelled constantly. But there had to be a couple of people in the bleachers who either didn't know that, or chose to ignore it.

Libby, looking flushed and irritated, failed to return a serve. John moved from the bench to hand Nicki a ball, but she had already pulled free the one in her pocket. She was just about to serve when she heard loud voices arguing. The voices sounded familiar. She allowed herself a slight turn of the head, just in time to see Deacon and Mel being escorted out by a security guard.

She lowered her arm. Great. Just great. They were the ones who had been making all the noise. And now her two staunchest supporters were being kicked out. Hadn't she warned Deacon about that? Why couldn't he have kept his mouth shut? Now they weren't even going to be there to see her win.

If she won.

She hoisted the racket with her right arm, prepared to serve.

Tossed the ball up in the air with her left hand.

The ball met the racket. And exploded.

Bright-red liquid poured down Nicki, coating her hair, her face, her neck and shoulders, burning her eyes, spilling down across her whites and her bare arms, splattering the floor around her.

Her mouth open in shock, Nicki stood alone on the tennis court, coated with a shiny, blood-red sheen.

Chapter 11

The spectators in the dome rose to their feet, letting out one collective gasp of horror. Then an appalled silence fell over the crowd.

For a few seconds, the entire dome froze, as if time had stopped.

Then Coach Dietch dropped the clipboard she was holding and dashed across the court to Nicki's side.

The other players left their courts, running to Nicki's side. Referees, linekeepers, and ball people gathered around her.

Nicki was only vaguely conscious of the activity, of people asking her questions, handing her towels, trying to help her wipe the slick, oily red from her eyes, her nose, her mouth. Pat was there, too, and she must have been saying something, because her mouth was open and her lips were moving, but Nicki heard nothing. She felt as if she had removed herself from the scene, as if she were watching the whole ugly mess through a window.

Someone took her elbow. Someone was forcing her to move, walking her forward, off the court. Her own movements were automatic, with no sense of direction or purpose. She simply followed where she was led.

"Why isn't she saying anything?" she heard then, a voice whispered from somewhere behind her. "Why isn't she crying? I would be."

Another voice said, "It's paint, you can smell it. Where'd it come from?"

And still another disembodied voice said, "It came from her ball. It was inside the ball she took out of her pocket. I saw her getting ready to serve, and tossing the ball up. She was about to win. One more point . . . but when she hit the ball, it exploded, and all that stuff came pouring down on her."

They're not real, Nicki thought numbly as she was led into the locker room, the voices aren't real. I'm imagining them. Because if the voices are real, then everything is real, and that can't be, that just can't be. I didn't walk off the tennis court all covered with red paint in front of the whole school. I couldn't have. That would be too horrible to bear.

But if it wasn't real, why did her eyes burn so, why did her lips taste of paint, why were her arms and hands covered with red?

Well, she told herself matter-of-factly, I'm imagining all of that, too. My arms aren't really the color of blood, and my eyes don't really burn. I'm asleep and I'm having a nightmare, that's all.

There was great comfort in the belief, and so she held onto it with all of her might, even when someone . . . Pat? Coach? began swabbing at her face with a warm, wet washcloth, wiping gently, talking soothingly.

Because it wasn't really happening, Nicki lay down on the table someone had led her to and relaxed, closing her mind to everything except the belief that she was dreaming.

The wiping of her face and arms and legs continued, as did the voices.

"I don't like this," one voice said. Coach? Coach was in her dream? Her nightmare? "The way she's acting. She's too quiet. I expected hysteria, but this . . ."

Another voice suggested calling a doctor, still another talked about taking someone to the infirmary.

Nicki supposed the someone they were discussing was her. It was really weird to hear people talking about her and know that whatever they were saying didn't matter because none of it was real.

"I wish she'd snap out of it," the first voice said worriedly.

I will, Nicki thought lazily, just as soon as I wake up. She thought about opening her eyes, just to test out her theory, but her lashes seemed to be stuck together, as if they'd been glued. Must have some of that red stuff on them, she thought dreamily. It'll be nice to wake up and have it gone.

Someone was yelling, from a distance. Angry. At her? No, at one of the voices, now saying firmly, "No, Deacon, you can't come in here. We've got our hands full. We're going to put her in the shower. We'll let you know when you can see her. Go away."

Deacon's voice stopped arguing.

Nicki was lifted off the table, carried somewhere, set on her feet. Her eyes were still closed, and although the kind, soft voices warned her, she wasn't quite sure what it was they were warning her about. She wasn't prepared for the sudden shock of warm water that streamed down upon her from above.

She had no choice then. How could she stay asleep with water pouring down over her?

When she opened her eyes, with great difficulty because of her sticky lashes, she was in a shower stall, still in her clothes, and she was staring through a curtain of water into the concerned eyes of two people. Coach Dietch and Patrice Weylen.

They looked so worried.

"It's okay," Nicki said gently. "Don't you get it? It was all just a bad dream. Thanks for waking me up. I'll be fine now. Can I come out of the shower?" And then, before they could answer, she lifted her head and looked straight into a small, rectangular mirror hanging on the shower wall facing her.

And screamed.

Because underneath the fine stream of water, her hair was coated with a thin veneer of red, her eyes were horribly swollen, the whites pink, the edges rimmed with red, her lashes thick with the red goop, her cheeks and nose a scarlet blur.

She kept screaming until they pulled her out of the shower.

The next thing Nicki was aware of was waking up in a quiet white cubicle. She knew immediately that she was in the infirmary, and that she was alone.

And she remembered everything. Reaching up to slam her serve into Libby's court, hoping this would be the point that would do it, hoping Libby wouldn't be able to return it . . .

Then the ball, exploding, the horrible red stuff splashing down upon her . . .

Nicki slid beneath the scratchy white blanket, shuddering in revulsion. All those people in the dome had seen it happen, had watched her being showered with red . . . red what? Paint, hadn't someone said? They had all seen her standing there, a big, red blob, frozen in place. They had all watched as she was led off the court, dripping scarlet.

She couldn't bear the thought. Tears of humiliation stung her sore eyes. She fought them back, trying to focus her thoughts.

How had paint got inside her tennis ball?

She was struggling to trace the path of the ball from the sporting-goods store to her gym bag to the locker room to John when the same security guard who had supervised the installation of a new lock on her door entered the cubicle. He was accompanied by Coach Dietch, Pat, and a white-faced Ginnie.

"It was paint, all right," he said, pulling a small notebook from his shirt pocket and flipping it open. "Thinned it with paint thinner first, that's why your eyes are such a mess. Looks like someone tried to blind you. You got lucky."

Lucky? Nicki sat up. "How did paint get inside my tennis ball?"

The man shrugged. "Could be someone took it apart, dumped the paint in, glued the pieces back together. Twin Falls police have a different theory, though. I talked to a fellow there, he says if they can find a hole in one of the ball fragments, it'll mean someone never took the ball apart at all, that they thinned the paint and then injected it into the ball using a hypodermic needle, one of those big ones, used for horses and cows. The weight of the paint made the ball burst when you hit it with your racket. The guy said he heard about something like that in a case in Australia, except that ball had carbon tetrachloride in it. Blinded the woman who hit it. I sent the ball fragments to Twin Falls. I'll let you know what they find out."

This time, he pressed Nicki repeatedly for information about who might have "pulled this stunt." But Nicki knew that it was much, much more than a simple "stunt." The paint thinner could easily have blinded her. Was probably meant to.

He hadn't killed her in the whirlpool, so now he was willing to settle for blinding her? As it was, the skin on her face and arms was burned, and stung fiercely. And her eyelashes wouldn't be the same for a good long time. She'd probably lost half of them to the scrubbing.

But she could think of nothing to tell the security guard. Nicki knew Libby didn't like her, and most of the team had refused to make her feel welcome. But this was not the work of someone who simply *disliked* Nicki Bledsoe.

The person who had done this had to hate her with a passion.

What had she done to make someone hate her so much?

Deacon and Mel were allowed in to see her then, and the others left, telling Nicki to get some rest.

She felt safe with Deacon and Mel. *They* didn't play tennis. And thanks to Deacon's big mouth, which had got them tossed out of the dome, they hadn't witnessed her humiliation, so she was more comfortable with them. She couldn't imagine what it was going to feel like when she left the infirmary and had to face the world. Gruesome. Everyone would be checking her out to see if any traces of red remained. She'd feel like a store display sitting behind a glass window.

Still, she wasn't about to stay in the infirmary. How could she feel safe in the place where Barb had died?

"She was *supposed* to be *you*," Nicki heard again, and shuddered.

"You're being sprung in the morning," Deacon said, as if he'd read her mind. "But no one will expect you to attend classes, or practice.

Especially not practice. How about if Mel and I cut and we all spend the day in the state park up the road? Leave the scene of the crime, so to speak? Abandon the halls of academia to commune with nature."

"You need some fresh air, Nicki," Mel agreed. "Your face is as white as that pillowcase."

My face is white, Nicki thought, because I happen to be scared to death. Because just a little while ago, it *wasn't* white, it was covered with sticky, smelly, bright-red paint. And someone did that to me on purpose. That is *very* scary.

But not as scary as almost being murdered. As being there when a teammate died.

"I *am* going to go to practice," she said emphatically, deciding at that very moment. "It's not like I'm hurt. I'm not. My pride is black and blue, but the rest of me is intact. If I don't show up, whoever put that red slop in my tennis ball will think he's scared me off."

"You're going to keep playing tennis?" Mel asked, disapproval in her voice. "After what they *did* to you?"

"We don't know *who* did it, Mel," Nicki said patiently. "And even if it was someone on the team, it was probably only one person. Everyone else, and Coach, will be expecting me to show up. And I intend to." I sound so tough, she thought, as the nurse came in and told Deacon and Mel they'd have to leave. But inside, I'm jelly.

The nurse gave her something to help clear up the painful skin rash caused by a combination of the paint and the scrubbing necessary to remove it, and a mild sedative to help her get a good night's sleep.

"You were in shock," the woman said, plumping Nicki's pillow. "Can't say that I blame you. I've seen some nasty things in my time, but this one takes the cake. Lucky you weren't blinded. Of course," she added innocently, "you were luckier than your friend was last week."

I know, I know, Nicki thought wearily. People keep telling me I'm a lucky girl.

As the nurse was leaving, she flicked the light switch, plunging the room into darkness.

Nicki bolted upright in bed. "Please, could you leave that on?" she cried. The whirlpool room, with its side door, was only steps away from where she lay. "I can't sleep with the lights off."

"The sedative will help you sleep," the nurse said, and didn't turn the lights back on.

"Please!" Nicki begged, feeling ridiculously childish. But if she didn't watch out for herself, who would? She needed the light *on*!

The nurse sighed. "After what you've been through today, I guess I can't blame you. I've got a nightlight here somewhere, let me look." A few minutes later, a soft, white light shone from the wall beside Nicki's bed. It wasn't much, but it was better than nothing. "Now, you go to sleep," the nurse said. "I'll be right outside. You're my only patient, and I'll keep a close eye on you, I promise. You're safe here."

Sure, Nicki thought bitterly. Hadn't she and Barb thought they were safe in the whirlpool? And they'd been wrong, hadn't they?

Fatally wrong.

She had planned to stay awake all night, her guard up against possible peril, keep her mind too busy to relax so she couldn't possibly fall asleep.

But her mind was as exhausted as her body, and the mild sedative sapped her determination. Then, too, her eyes stung less when the lids were closed. Maybe she'd just close them while she did her thinking. Thinking might even be easier with her eyes closed. Easier to concentrate.

"Nicole?" a voice called softly.

Nicki lifted her head, her eyelids heavy.

A figure stood in the doorway, holding something up in the air. At first, she thought it was another hairdryer, and her fogged mind struggled to think what harm it could do, when there was no water anywhere in her little cubicle.

But it wasn't a hairdryer, she realized. It . . . was . . . a . . . racket. A tennis racket. The hallway outside her room was dark, but she could see a dim outline in the reflected glow from her nightlight. A tennis racket, held high in the right hand of the figure in the doorway.

"You do love tennis, don't you, Nicole?" the voice whispered, swinging the racket over his head, as if he were getting ready to serve. "You want to play tennis, don't you? But the thing is, Nicole, you don't deserve to have what you want. Not after what you did."

"I . . . I didn't do anything," she protested weakly, trying to shrink down beneath the covers. "What did I do?"

There was a short, brittle laugh from the doorway. "You don't even know, do you? It means nothing to you. I wish *I* could feel that way. But, you see, I can't. Impossible. Why don't you *think*, Nicole? I've been trying to give you little hints. Because if you think of what it might be that you've done, maybe you'll have the decency to be sorry. That just *might* save your life."

Nicki reached out for the call button. Her hand hit the glass of water by the bed, knocking it over.

"No," she whispered. Her groping fingers found the call button.

"That's right Nicki. Call for help. You're going to need it. You're going to need all the help you can get."

When the nurse arrived, Nicki babbled hysterically, trying to explain what had happened.

"Why, there's no one here but you and me," the nurse said, gently pushing Nicki back down onto the pillow. "No one came in. I'd have seen them. You must have had a bad dream. The medication does that sometimes."

She sounded so absolutely sure, so positive, that after a while, Nicki decided it had been a bad dream. Like the other night . . .

It had to have been a dream. Because although she tried, for just a few sleepy minutes before closing her eyes for the last time that night, to remember something awful that she had done, nothing came to mind.

If there *was* something, she'd remember. Wouldn't she?

Chapter 12

Waiting to be released the following morning, Nicki thought about quitting tennis. In spite of her bravado telling Deacon and Mel about showing up at practice, the thought of walking into the dome again made her skin crawl.

The dome wasn't safe.

For just a moment, she wished she could stay in the infirmary, curled up in a nice, safe ball under the scratchy white blanket.

Then she remembered the whirlpool, just down the hall. This place wasn't any safer than the dome. She couldn't stay here.

And she couldn't give up tennis. She had made a commitment to Coach Dietch, and to the team. And there was her scholarship. She couldn't toss that away like a used tissue. She needed it.

On the other hand, she argued mentally,

what good would a scholarship do her if she were blinded . . . or worse?

Good question.

The arrival of Pat and Ginnie with clean clothes for her, ended Nicki's silent argument with herself.

As she went through her normal Monday routine, she was relieved to find that no one seemed to be staring or pointing at her. Maybe because she looked perfectly normal now that she was no longer dripping with red. And if they were whispering about her, they weren't being obvious about it.

An even bigger surprise came when she arrived at practice. Half the squad surrounded her the minute she stepped into the dome.

They asked her how she felt.

They wanted to know if her eyes were all right.

A girl named Sara asked if Nicki needed to borrow anything, and a girl named Joanie wanted to know if the whites Nicki had been wearing on Sunday were ruined.

The unexpected reception dumbfounded Nicki.

She didn't know exactly what she *had* expected, but it certainly wasn't this. It was . . . nice.

Still, even as she answered all the questions,

she was acutely aware of Libby and Libby's followers huddling in a distant corner of the dome. Libby did not look pleased by the attention being given Nicki.

When John arrived at the dome, he headed straight for Nicki's group. Ginnie joined them a few minutes later, and more and more people began gravitating in that direction.

It was all too much for Libby. She threw her racket onto a bench in disgust and stormed out of the dome.

Watching her leave, Hannah said firmly, "I think *she* did it. I think Libby's the one who put that red stuff in your ball, Nicki. She really hates you."

Ginnie disagreed. "She's too competitive. She wouldn't wreck a match that way. Now she can't be sure she would have won yesterday. And she has to know that no one else is sure, either. It must be driving her crazy. Besides," Ginnie added laconically, "Libby would never electrocute someone."

Nicki wasn't convinced. "Crazy" being the operative word. Maybe Libby wouldn't do terrible things when she was thinking clearly. But what if she was so angry about Nicki's presence on the team that she was no longer thinking rationally? That would make a difference, wouldn't it?

Several times during practice that day, Nicki glanced over at Libby and shivered as she saw the brute force with which Libby slammed the ball back across the net.

She wishes that were me, Nicki thought with absolute conviction. Libby would be in seventh heaven if she could just smash me back and forth across the net like that.

It was a sobering thought.

Even more sobering was the sight of the large, blood-red stain on the court in the spot where Nicki had been standing the day before when her ball burst. An understanding Coach Dietch had assigned Nicki to a different court. But Nicki had seen it when she first walked into the dome, knew it was there. And was painfully aware of it throughout practice.

Still, buoyed by the sudden, unexpected support from much of the team, she played remarkably well that afternoon. She reveled in the resulting praise as they all walked off the courts and headed for the locker rooms. The atmosphere was *so* different from what it had been, Nicki could almost feel happy.

In spite of Libby. In spite of everything.

"Come eat with us," Sara invited. "We're going over to Burgers Etc. It'll be fun. We won't even talk tennis if you don't want."

"I don't mind talking tennis." Better than

talking about Barb, or the horrible ball filled with paint and paint thinner. "And I'll come, but I'm bringing Pat and Ginnie, okay?" She wasn't about to forget the only two people who'd befriended her from the start.

"Sure. Whatever."

Ginnie and Pat were delighted, at first. Then, as they were drying their hair after their showers, Pat came up behind Nicki and said anxiously, "Are you sure this is a good idea? For all we know, one of those people is out to get you. Do you really think it's safe to be around them?"

"Pat," Nicki answered, shaking her hair into place, "I don't know what's going on. Not a clue. But I do know that I have to eat. And nothing terrible can happen to me in a public place like Burgers Etc."

"Oh, I don't know." Pat brushed her own short hair back behind her ears. "If they can get at your tennis ball and put paint in it, why can't they put poison in your burger?"

She said it lightly, but Nicki knew she was only half-kidding. Forcing a laugh that came out as a nervous, humorless sound, she replied, "Great! You just ruined my appetite. Everything I eat is going to taste weird now."

But it didn't. Everything tasted great, because in spite of the past few horrific days, she was sitting in a popular college restaurant with a large group of people, and it was fun. She hadn't forgotten that something was very wrong. How could she? But there was nothing she could do about it, not yet, not now. So why not enjoy the moment while she had it?

She did find herself, more than once, glancing around the overcrowded booth at the laughing, animated faces, wondering if one of them could belong to the shadowy figure behind the whirlpool. But it seemed impossible. That figure had been so menacing. No one at the table seemed the least bit threatening.

Except Libby, of course, who stopped by Nicki's booth on her way out of the diner to lean over the table and say, "It almost looks like whoever sabotaged that ball of yours did you a favor, doesn't it? I mean, suddenly you're *so* popular."

When Nicki refused to answer, Libby shrugged and moved away from the table, calling over her shoulder, "Maybe you did it yourself, Nicki. Doctored that tennis ball. Great way of getting attention." She was laughing as one of her followers held the door open for her. Everyone at Nicki's table grew quiet.

"She doesn't really think I would do something that stupid, does she?" Nicki said, glancing around at the faces in her booth.

"Of course not," Pat was the first to answer. "She's just yanking your chain. Trying to get a rise out of you."

"Well, it worked." Nicki stared glumly at her half-eaten hamburger.

"Don't let her get to you," Ginnie said. "She probably just said that to throw suspicion off herself. A lot of people think she did it."

There were nods all around the table.

Ginnie quickly added, "Except me. I've said it before, and I'll say it again. It wasn't her."

Nicki glanced at her with suspicion. "You seem awfully sure. Do you know something we don't?"

Ginnie's eyes darkened angrily. "If I did, I'd tell you. She just wouldn't do that kind of thing, that's all."

"Why," Sara asked, "because she's such a good sport? We've all seen her throw her racket, more than once. Maybe she doesn't know how much damage that can do, but I do."

Everyone looked at Sara with interest.

"I was in the Tri-State regional championships at Forest Hills when I was twelve . . ." she began.

"You were?" Nicki interrupted in surprsie. "So was I! We were living back here then, in Nokomis, New York. In fact, we were moving the next day to Denver. I don't remember you, though, Sara. Sorry."

There were other nods around the table. Several of them had lived in the area at the time and had played in that tournament.

"There were tons of kids there," Sara continued. "I wouldn't expect you to remember me. What I started to say was, I heard that after the tournament, some kid was partially blinded by a stone that hit his eye when a tennis brat who'd lost that night threw a racket on a patch of gravel. So Libby ought to be more careful, that's all." Having finished her story, Sara paused, then said, "Nicki? What's the matter? Your face is dead white."

Everyone's attention switched to Nicki. Her face was indeed pale and chalky, her eyes open wide and staring at Ginnie. "What are you *talking* about?" she said, her voice hoarse with anxiety. "Someone lost an eye?"

"Oh, well, I don't know that someone *lost* an eye. Only that a kid was hit in the eye with a stone and his eye had been injured. But before we left the next day to go back home, my father heard that the kid probably wouldn't be able to see out of that eye again, and so wouldn't be able to play tennis anymore. I remember that, because I thought it would be so horrible.

I'm surprised you didn't hear about it then, if you were there."

"I told you," Nicki said. "We were moving the next day. We drove back home that night and left for Denver the next morning. I never heard anything about it. It's . . . it's revolting. Blinded? By a stone?"

"Not completely blinded," Pat pointed out. "I mean, I know it's horrible, but Sara said it was one eye, not both. Nicki, what's *wrong* with you? Are you okay?"

No, she wasn't okay. Nicki was definitely not okay. "Do . . . do you know who it was? The kid who was hit by the stone, I mean?" she asked Sara.

"No."

"Girl or boy?" Nicki persisted.

"I told you, I don't know. What difference does it make? All I know is, someone who was so good at tennis that he — or she — made it to the tournament, probably never got to play again."

Nicki moaned softly, and put a hand over her eyes.

Everyone at the table exchanged worried glances. "Nicki?" Pat said. "It was a long time ago."

Yes, Nicki knew that. Six years. Six years ago. Now it was coming back to haunt her, after all this time, like the Ghost of Christmas Past.

She slid down in the booth, her hand over her eyes, so dizzy and nauseated she was afraid she was going to pass out, right there in front of everyone. And then she remembered.

It was June, early summer, with the trees fully leafed out and the sun, as they arrived at the tournament, warming the courts. A beautiful day. But the Bledsoe family was moving again the next day, and Nicki was furious about it. She loved living in Nokomis. It was the best place they'd ever lived. And now, her parents were taking her away again. She hated them for it.

But since she had no choice, and had to leave, it seemed important that she go out in a blaze of glory. So she was determined to win.

But she didn't. She lost, big time. And left the stadium that night quivering with disappointment and fury. Left after dark in the middle of a huge crowd, walking with her head down, swinging her racket angrily. Her parents were waiting for her in the car, five minutes away. She decided she was never going to play tennis again. That would show her parents how angry she really was. It was a stupid game, anyway.

Her fury took over, and she threw her racket to the ground. The walkway they were on was gravel, full of small stones. The racket sent a handful of stones flying up in every direction, hitting people. Nicki didn't see what happened, but a child somewhere behind her screamed, a blood-chilling shriek. Then a woman cried, "Terry, Terry, what's the matter?" and a second later, shouted, "Oh, my god, what's happened to your eye?"

Nicki scooped up her racket and raced all the way to the car. She jumped in and told her father she had to go the bathroom really bad, so could he please hurry?

By the next day, she knew she had to tell someone. She had to know what had happened after she ran away. She told her father.

He called the stadium to see if anything had been reported, but no one there knew anything. Then he called area hospitals, with no luck. It was getting late, and they had to leave ahead of the moving van. Her father decided the injury must have been a minor one and gave her a long lecture about never throwing her racket, a lecture she no longer needed. She had learned her lesson.

She never heard any more about the incident. It had never occurred to her that because of it, someone who loved the game of tennis might never have played it again after that night.

But now, after what Sara had said, Nicki, dread choking her, remembered other things . . . like how white her father's face had been when he hung up after talking to one of the hospitals. She had told herself then that he was white with relief, but now . . . had that been when he found out the truth? A truth so shocking that it had drained the color from his face?

And her parents had argued all that morning. She had blamed that on the stress of moving. But they had moved many times before, and they'd never argued so vehemently. She remembered her mother whispering harshly, when she thought Nicki wasn't close enough to hear, "You can't tell her, you can't!" And what was it that her father had responded? Something about Nicki needing to "know the truth."

She had thought they'd meant that the house in Denver wasn't as nice as the one in Nokomis, or that maybe the school was horrible.

So, when she got to Denver and the house and the school was fine, maybe even nicer than in Nokomis, why hadn't she asked herself what that argument had really been about?

Because she was afraid.

Because she didn't want to know the "truth" that her father had talked about.

There had been letters, too. Long, white official-looking envelopes with the return address of a New York law firm printed in the upper left-hand corner. They'd been in the mail when Nicki collected it on cold, snowy Colorado days. Her mother had said they had to do with the sale of their New York house.

Had her parents been sued because of what she'd done?

Was Terry short for Terrence, or Teresa?

He or she hadn't been from Nokomis. She knew every tennis player in Nokomis. No one named Terry played tennis in her town.

But there had been kids from three states at Forest Hills.

Nicki heard again the words, "After what you did," coming from the voice of the shadowy figure in the infirmary doorway.

No . . . ridiculous . . . crazy . . . that had been six years ago, and no one knew who she was. She had grabbed up her racket and run. No one knew it was her fault. The words spoken in the infirmary couldn't possibly have anything to do with that incident.

How could her parents have kept the truth from her? Why hadn't they told her? How could they have lied to her all these years?

Everyone at the table was staring at her.

"They never found out who threw that racket?" Nicki asked Sara.

"I don't know. Probably. I mean, isn't that

always the first question parents ask when someone gets hurt? Who did it? They always want to know who did it and how it happened, as if that would change anything. But I never heard who it was."

That's because it was covered up, Nicki thought bitterly. The truth was carefully hidden, so you couldn't see it.

She had to get out of there. Taking a deep breath, she managed to stand up. "I need to leave now," she said.

No one argued with her. They could see how shaken she was. She knew they thought it was simply the thought of a tennis player no longer able to play the game he or she must have loved. She was willing to let them think that. She couldn't bring herself to tell them what she now believed to be the truth.

Chapter 13

The first thing Nicki did when she got back to her room was call her parents. Nicki's mother answered the telephone and her father picked up the extension in the living room. When they had all exchanged greetings, Nicki said, as casually as she could manage, "Do you two remember when we were living back here, in Nokomis, and I played in that big tri-state tournament the night before we moved to Denver?"

The silence that followed told her everything. Her worst fears were confirmed. It was true. It was all true, and they'd known this whole time. They had kept the truth from her.

Her father cleared his throat. "Nicki, you've been in so many tournaments."

"Don't," she murmured in a strangled voice, "don't keep it up. I *know*. Why didn't you *tell* me?" She was sitting on her bed, and now she sagged back against the wall. "I don't understand."

Another silence. Then her mother said, "Nicki, why are you thinking about that night now, after all this time?"

But Nicholas Bledsoe said in a weary voice, "Give it up, Celeste. We knew there was a good chance she'd hear something when we moved back east. Nicki's right. It's time to quit pretending." To his daughter, he said quietly, "What do you need to know?"

She didn't know where to begin. So many questions. So many awful answers, waiting to be spoken aloud. "Did that child really lose the sight in one eye?"

Her father cleared his throat. "Yes. But," he added quickly, "it was an accident, Nicki. No one blamed you."

Someone did, she thought. Someone who had said, "After what you did. . . ."

"You told me you didn't find out anything," Nicki accused. "You said there hadn't been any reports of an accident like that."

"We felt it was for your own good, Nicole." Her mother's voice, low and calm. "It was an *accident*, honey. We couldn't see what good it would do for you to know. Your father paid all of the child's medical bills, every penny."

The letters from the New York law firm.

Nicki felt sick again. "Oh, God," she groaned, bending double on her bed. The room was spinning around her, a pale blue blur. "Oh, no, no. I *didn't* do that, I didn't. Someone is blind in one eye because of *me*?"

Her father's voice, deep and suddenly stern, came back on the line. "Nicole, listen to me. I don't know why you've dredged up this thing after all these years, but I wouldn't have told you if I didn't think you could handle it like an adult. Don't prove me wrong now. As your mother said, it was an unfortunate accident, and it was handled in the best way possible. There is no sense at all in dwelling on it now, after all this time."

"Terry . . ." Nicki murmured. "The name that woman screamed was Terry. Did I blind a girl or a boy?"

Her mother gasped at her daughter's choice of words. "You didn't blind anyone!" she said angrily. "Not . . . not completely. Don't say that!"

"Was it a girl or a boy?" Nicki demanded furiously. Beads of cold sweat stood out on her forehead.

"We don't know," her father answered finally. "They never said, and we never asked. We dealt only with the family's lawyers, and they referred to the child only as 'minor child Gideon.' So we don't know."

Gideon? Terry Gideon. Terrence Gideon. Teresa Gideon.

She didn't know anyone whose last name was Gideon.

"Was 'minor child Gideon' a good tennis player?" she asked harshly. "Or just mediocre?"

"Nicki . . ."

"Answer me! Was he a really *good* tennis player? Someone with the potential to be a champion, maybe?"

Her father sighed heavily. "Yes, I guess you could say that. From what the lawyer said, yes, the child was on the way to becoming a tennis champion. They probably could have used that to bring a lawsuit against us, but the parents weren't that kind of people. They asked nothing of us beyond the medical bills."

The person she'd injured had been good enough to become a champion?

The operative words there being "had been," Nicki reflected bitterly. Past tense after her temper tantrum. Because you could do many, many things with only one eye, but playing tennis wouldn't be one of them.

"Please, dear," her mother begged, "don't be angry with us. You were only twelve years old. And you were already having problems because of the frequent moving. We saw no point in adding to those problems by giving you the burden of guilt over a terrible accident. You can understand that, can't you?"

Nicki knew that if she hung up without saying she understood, neither one of them would have a moment's rest. They had meant well, she knew that. They'd done it to protect their only child from a lifetime of nightmares.

But their deception had been useless, after all. Because the nightmare had come to haunt her — here at Salem. Now, for the first time, she knew why.

It was hard, not telling them what was going on on campus. But they couldn't do anything about it, and she wasn't yet willing to give up and go home. If she told them about Barb's death and the paint episode, they'd whisk her out of the university so fast, her hair would curl.

"It's okay, Mom," she said numbly. "It's okay, really. If I didn't want to hear the answer, I shouldn't have asked the question."

"I still don't understand why you did," her father said. "Why now, after all this time?"

"I had a nightmare about it," she answered truthfully. She must have cried out the words, "I'm sorry" in her sleep because some small part of her knew, and had always known, the truth. That a child wouldn't have screamed like that if there hadn't been some serious damage.

Hadn't she always known, somewhere deep inside of her, that her father's face wouldn't have been so white if he'd found out nothing from the hospitals, and that the arguing, which she now realized had been over whether or not to tell her the truth, wasn't just about moving? Hadn't she known?

She'd lied to herself just as much as they had lied to her.

"Nicki," her father said, "should we come up there? You don't sound right. We shouldn't have told you over the phone. But it was so long ago, I thought . . . well, I thought it would be all right."

It *was* long ago. But what her parents were forgetting was, for their daughter it might as well have happened today, because today was when she found out about it. It was old to *them*, because they'd known all this time. But it was new to her. New, and horrible.

"Don't be silly, dad," she said, forcing her voice to stay steady. "I'm fine. I'm shocked, of course. Who wouldn't be?" She did *not* want them driving up to Salem now. Not now. "But I'm okay with it. I promise I won't blow it all out of proportion." As if that were possible. As if that could ever be possible. What *was* the proper proportion for the kind of news she'd just received?

It took her another ten minutes to convince them that she really was okay. They finally let her hang up.

She felt sorry for them. All these years, they'd kept the whole awful business to themselves, probably always wondering if they'd done the right thing by not telling her.

She shouldn't judge them. Maybe they'd been right. She'd been such a mess then, again and again having to leave a place she loved, not sleeping or eating for weeks after they arrived in the new place, snapping at everyone, glaring at her parents with raw hatred. Until she began playing tennis again. Then things went back to normal, at least until it came time to pack again.

So, maybe they'd known her better than she knew herself.

She lay down on the bed, her hands over her eyes. Now that she knew, what was she supposed to do with this? What good did it do her to know?

Someone knocked on the door.

"Go away!" she called, not getting up.

"No," Pat's voice answered. And Ginnie's

followed with, "Nicki, let us in. We're worried about you."

Nicki sighed. They were trying to help. She got up and went to let them in.

"We were really worried," Pat said, dropping to the floor to sit. "You were acting so weird. Not that I blame you. You okay?"

Ginnie sat beside Pat on the floor. "What's up, Nicole?"

She sat down on the bed. And then she told them. The whole, ugly story. If they were so shocked and disgusted that they hated her, she would just have to live with that. But she couldn't keep something like this to herself. She couldn't.

When she had finished, Ginnie said, "No wonder you were so upset. Gee, Nicki, I'm really sorry. Sara would never have brought it up if she'd known you were involved."

"Not her fault," Nicki said firmly. "I didn't know it myself. I'm glad I know now. It explains a lot of things. I just don't know what to do with it now that I know."

They were all silent for a bit, and then Ginnie asked, "The kid who was hit with the stone was from around here somewhere?"

Nicki shrugged. "I guess so. New York, New Jersey, or Pennsylvania. Why?"

"I know what she's thinking," Pat said.

"She's thinking about the ball with the paint in it, aren't you, Ginnie?"

Ginnie nodded.

"And the whirlpool," Pat said, "There's the whirlpool thing, too. You did say, Nicki, that the hairdryer was meant for you."

Ginnie thought for a minute before saying to Nicki, "Maybe you ought to think about who you know that has trouble with one eye."

"But that's crazy! It was six years ago. And no one even knew it was me," Nicki insisted.

"Sure, they did," Pat argued. "You said your parents sent money, right? They had to send the checks, didn't they? The kid could have seen the name on them. Or he could have found out some other way. But my guess is, he did find out."

Nicki thought about that. She knew people who wore contacts . . . Ginnie, Pat, Sara . . . But she didn't know anyone who had only partial vision. Because, of course, someone like that wouldn't be *able* to play tennis, would they? Might not even be able to *watch* a match, either. Or drive a car or play any sport that required peripheral vision, would probably even have difficulty reading.

Maybe it wasn't so crazy to think that someone wanted revenge for an accident that had taken place six years before.

"You weren't living around here," Pat said, "so he couldn't get at you. But now you're here, and maybe he is, too. Maybe the person who got hit by that stone has been waiting all this time for you."

When Nicki pressed, "How would he even know I was here?' Ginnie reminded her that while she was at State, her name had been seen on the sports pages more than once. "Anyone in the area could have seen it."

At last they left. But soon another rap on her door startled her, pulling her out of her morbid thoughts.

Why couldn't people just leave her alone right now?

She opened the door to Deacon and Mel.

"Do you know anyone on campus named Gideon?" Nicki burst out before they'd even stepped inside the room. "Is there anyone in any of your classes whose last name is Gideon?"

"Well, hi to you, too," Deacon said, ambling past her to sink into her desk chair.

Mel, flopping down on Nicki's bed, said lazily, "*What* an unusual greeting. You're so creative, Nicki."

"Well, *do* you?" Nicki demanded.

They both shook their heads. "Not I," Mel said, leaning back against the wall. "Why? Are you on a Gideon hunt? What's a gideon, any-way? Is it like a holy grail?"

Nicki was about to tell them when something stopped her. Pretending to be fumbling with the lock on her door, she kept her back to them as her mind raced. She didn't know if her friends' theory about revenge was valid or not. But it could be. And if it was, *anyone* on campus could be the grown-up Gideon child. *Anyone*. Deacon could be Terrence Gideon. How many guys in this world are named Deacon, anyway? He could have made up that name himself, so that no one, especially her, would know who he really was.

Or . . . Mel could be Teresa Gideon.

Wasn't it, after all, pretty weird that they'd come along when she'd had that flat tire? As if . . . as if they'd been following her. As if they'd known all along that her tire was going to go flat. And although neither played tennis, they went to all the matches. Didn't that show a love of the sport that could have come from playing the game as a child? Loving it as a child?

If Mel *was* the adult Gideon child, Deacon could be helping her seek revenge, because they were friends.

If the revenge theory wasn't totally off the wall.

She mumbled some lame excuse about her question, telling them to forget it, and they seemed to accept that.

Her suspicions made her sick. She liked Deacon and Mel. And they had been friendly to her when almost no one else had been.

But maybe, just maybe, they'd had an ulterior motive for their friendship.

"Are you memorizing that lock?" Deacon asked drily. "They're all pretty much the same, Nicki. No distinguishing characteristics to tell one from the other, as far as I know."

Funny he should mention that, because when she turned around, the first thing she intended to do was search their faces carefully, as surreptitiously as possible, for any sign that they'd ever ended up in a hospital emergency room in Forest Hills, New York, with blood streaming from an injured eye. Nicki wasn't even sure what to look for. A small scar, maybe, around the eye area? A way of turning the head completely to look at something off to one side, instead of merely glancing in that direction as most people would do?

Surely she'd be able to tell if one of them had less than full vision. Wouldn't she?

But although they were in her room for nearly half an hour, and although Mel was lounging off to Deacon's left side, and although

Nicki observed carefully, she saw no sign that either had impaired vision. When Deacon spoke to Mel, he didn't turn his head completely, but simply glanced in her direction. It was harder to tell in Mel's case, because both Nicki and Deacon were seated before her, which meant Mel didn't have to glance sideways.

The strain was getting to Nicki. She finally told them she was tired and needed to sleep.

"I hate athletes," Mel complained, standing up. "They're no fun. Always in training, always sleeping or scarfing down carbohydrates, or practicing. We were going to go down and walk across the railroad bridge in the moonlight. Full moon, Nicki, shining down on the river. It'll be really awesome. You sure you won't come?"

"That rickety old bridge behind campus? I thought that was off-limits, Mel. Unsafe. I was warned about that bridge when I first got here." Going to the bridge this late at night seemed even odder to Nicki than most of Deacon and Mel's activities. Or . . . was there some specific reason why they wanted Nicki to go with them to such a dangerous place?

Nicki's skin crawled. She tried to push the nasty thought away.

Mel laughed. The long, heavy, silver earrings she was wearing jiggled precariously.

"Off-limits? Nicki, what exactly does that *mean?* Will we be spanked and sent to our rooms if we're caught? Given detention? Put on a diet of bread and water? Honestly, Nicki, life is too short to let people set limits for you. You should set your own."

Nicki felt herself flushing. She wasn't anything like the two of them. Why were Deacon and Mel even interested in her? Wasn't that suspicious? What *were* they doing becoming friends with her, anyway?

Maybe she had made a mistake, asking them if they knew anyone named Gideon. Because if one of them was Terry Gideon, they knew now that Nicki suspected the connection between that night at Forest Hills and what was happening to her now at Salem.

"Well, my own limits don't include challenging a dangerous old railroad bridge," Nicki said, moving to the door to open it. "Sorry."

Deacon hung back in the doorway as Mel left the room and began walking down the hall. "Sure you won't join us in our nocturnal adventure?" he asked, reaching out to lightly trace a finger along Nicki's cheek. "Could be interesting."

"I'm sure." His hand was warm. So were his eyes, dark as the night. "But everyone was really nice at practice today, and I played better than I have since I got here. I don't want to blow my new image by dragging into the dome too tired to return a serve."

His hand left her face and his eyes lost their warmth. "Right," he said curtly. "What was I thinking? Your teammates have all treated you so splendidly, you certainly owe them a great debt. Wouldn't want to disappoint them. They'd be crushed."

"Deacon . . ."

But he was already striding away from the door, calling out to Mel.

Nicki told herself that it probably meant nothing when Mel stopped and turned completely around at the sound of Deacon's voice, instead of simply glancing over her shoulder as most people would have done. People, for instance, with full vision in both eyes.

Mel was probably just being polite. Waiting for Deacon, instead of tossing a look over her shoulder to show that she'd heard while continuing to walk down the hallway.

Even though one label Nicki would never have used for Mel was "polite."

Nicki closed the door and locked it.

Chapter 14

After hours of agonized thought, Nicki decided to go to the security officer to tell him about Terrence or Teresa Gideon. When she had done that and suggested that he find out if someone by that name was on campus, she felt some sense of relief. She knew telling him didn't make her safe. But at least, something was being done.

Nothing threatening had happened since the paint episode. Nicki began to allow herself to hope that it was over. Whatever Barb's killer had been trying to do, it hadn't worked, and so he'd given up.

She would almost convince herself. And then a cold tingling sensation up her spine would tell her that it wasn't true. It wasn't over. She wasn't safe.

Her mind bounced back and forth like a tennis ball, was she safe, wasn't she, yes she was, no she wasn't. In spite of her nerves being drawn as taut as the strings on her racket, she continued to play well at practice. Admiration for her skill grew among the team members. Now, when her towel was snatched and hidden while she was in the shower, her hairbrush dipped in liquid soap, she knew she was being welcomed in the usual way. Finally.

If it had happened earlier, when she first arrived, she would have enjoyed it totally. It was harder now, knowing that while many of the team members had accepted her, there was still someone out there, somewhere, who hated her.

The down side of doing so well at practice, and being accepted by the other players was, she was either too tired at night to go out with Deacon and Mel, or she had already made plans to eat with, and maybe hang out with afterward, people from the team and John Silver. Sometimes, Deacon and Mel arrived after practice to join Nicki and her new friends. But more often, they knew nothing about Nicki's plans in time to join her. On those nights, they were either waiting impatiently for her in the hall when she returned to her room, or Deacon called after she was in bed to complain that she was avoiding them.

Well, maybe she was. Because Deacon and

Mel didn't play tennis? Deacon had said he'd played, once upon a time, but no longer did. With the exception of Libby and her followers, Nicki felt safe now only with people who *did* play tennis, because that meant they had full vision in both eyes . . . and no reason to hate Nicole Bledsoe. The people she couldn't be sure of were the ones who *didn't* play. Deacon and Mel *didn't*.

Still, she missed Deacon, more than she'd expected to.

She was pleased to notice that John and Ginnie were getting along well and spending a lot of time together. John was such a nice person. And Pat didn't seem to mind their new closeness, probably because she was included in the larger group now and was as busy as Nicki.

The security guard had called her on Wednesday to say there was no one named Gideon on the campus of Salem University, but added that he was still "looking into the matter." "Could be someone living in Twin Falls, working, not going to school," he had said in a matter-of-fact voice.

Could be. But the killer certainly knew his way around campus.

On Friday after practice, Coach Dietch called Nicki into her office to congratulate her on her performance during the week. "I knew

I was right about you," she said when Nicki had closed the door. "I really must thank John."

Nicki took a seat opposite Coach's desk. "John?"

"John Silver." Coach gave Nicki an inquiring look. "Oh, didn't you know? I've seen you talking to him at practice, so I assumed he'd told you. John is the one who told me about you. Said he'd seen you play and thought it would be worth my while to go up to State and take a look. John knows his tennis, so I went. And," giving Nicki a smile, "John was right. As usual."

"John? John Silver told you about me?" Nicki thought about that. He hadn't said a word, not even that first night when she'd told him about her full scholarship. John was responsible for that?

She would have to thank him. Funny he'd never mentioned his part in her coming to Salem. But maybe he was shy about it.

When Coach asked Nicki if she was "feeling better," Nicki couldn't answer honestly, "Yes." She said instead, "As long as I'm playing okay, I'll be all right."

That seemed to satisfy Coach, who never mentioned Barb.

Nicki was grateful. She still couldn't stand the thought of talking about the dead girl.

Nothing anyone said could change the terrible facts.

By the time she left the office, everyone else had already taken their showers. Nicki thought briefly of waiting until she got back to her room to take her own shower, and quickly decided against it. On a Friday night, the showers on her floor at Devereaux would be packed with partygoers. She'd have the showers all to herself.

She regretted that decision the moment she stepped out of the shower and not only found herself alone in the locker room, but alone in the dark. Someone who hadn't heard the water running must have thought everyone had gone, and had turned off all of the overhead fluorescent lights.

I've been so careful not to be anywhere alone, Nicki thought uneasily. And now, here I am, alone in the dark, which is exactly where I don't want to be.

She tilted her head to listen for sounds, and heard none. No stealthy footsteps, no furtive breathing. She really *was* alone. So . . . maybe she was okay.

Dressing quickly in the jeans, sweater, and sneakers she'd piled on a bench outside the shower cubicle, Nicki carefully made her way through the darkness to her locker, wishing she had accepted Pat's and Ginnie's offer to wait for her. But they had said she'd have to hurry because Ginnie wanted to get to the mall, where they were meeting John for dinner. Nicki had told them to go on ahead, that she'd meet them there. Big mistake? she wondered as she felt along the metal lockers for her own. A dark, quiet, deserted locker room was very different from a crowded, noisy, well-lit locker room. Had an entirely different feel to it. Not a good feeling at all.

Take the people out of a place, she thought, and it dies. Without people, every place must seem dead. Still and silent and cold, yet not really peaceful.

Because her locker was at the end of the row, directly opposite and below a tall, skinny window, the light from outside made it easier to find. Twenty-three. Right where she'd left it.

But . . . different . . .

Nicki stopped halfway there. She could see now . . . the wall of tall, wide khaki-colored lockers bathed in a diffused glow from the window . . . and there, at the end, number twenty-three . . .

Something was hanging on the door.

What was hanging on her locker door was something she'd seen before. But that time, it had been hanging from the light fixture in her room.

A shredded tennis racket, its sliced strings splaying outward, leaving a gaping hole in the center.

Even before she reached the locker, she knew with absolute conviction that this time, the racket was her own.

Breathing unevenly, she moved forward slowly, her eyes glancing around fearfully for some sign of the vandal who had committed this latest atrocity. She saw no one, heard no telltale sound.

But he couldn't have hung the racket until everyone else had left the locker room. That wasn't more than ten or fifteen minutes ago. He could still be here, hiding.

If he *was* here, *she* shouldn't be.

Without touching the racket, Nicki whirled and ran, racing for the door, which seemed to be miles and miles away, at the other end of the locker room.

And it seemed, too, to take her hours to reach it. Twice, she banged a knee on a bench. She slipped once, on the tile, and almost fell. But she kept going, her hands outstretched in front of her to feel for obstacles in her path.

When she finally, finally, reached the door, she was breathing hard. Her hand flew out to grasp the curved handle and pull the door open.

It didn't open. It didn't move. Didn't even edge forward a little to prove that it was just stuck, not locked.

That was because the door *was* locked, Nicki realized with a dangerous lurch of her heart when she had pulled and tugged and kicked with all her might, in vain.

Nicki couldn't get out of the locker room.

She was trapped in this cold, dead, silent place.

Chapter 15

Nicki, her heart flip-flopping in her chest, leaned against the door. She hated to leave it. It seemed safer here, so close to freedom. If she could only get the door open. But she couldn't. She had tried, and tried. It was closed as tightly against her as the door of a bank vault.

She listened again for any sound that would mean she had company in the locker room, and heard nothing. She breathed a bit easier.

Her hand moved along the door frame, slid sideways to the wall, exploring, found the light switch, flipped it.

Nothing happened.

Someone had done something to the electricity in this room. Someone had seen to it that Nicki would be in the dark. The same someone who had seen to it that she couldn't open the door and leave.

If someone had done all of that, wouldn't they want to hang around and watch her panic? They wouldn't leave, would they, and miss all the fun?

She had to clench her jaw to keep from screaming.

She tilted her head, listening. Nothing. Not even the smallest of sounds to tell her whether or not she was alone. The only noise she heard was the ragged sound of her own breathing.

But he was in here. She knew it. She wasn't alone.

She couldn't stay by the door. He'd come looking for her here, knowing she would be trying to escape.

Where could she go? Coach's office? No, it would be locked. And there was no other exit. Was there?

Stop it, Nicki told herself. Don't panic. *Think*.

She didn't remember seeing another door. But the locker room was pretty big to have only one exit. Weren't there fire laws or something that made the school put at least two exits in a room this size?

She would have to look. She would have to leave the door, so close to freedom, and dive into the dark depths of the locker room, searching for a way out.

Nicki peered into the darkness with its shadowy walls of tall, boxy lockers. If he was in there somewhere, waiting for her, she'd be playing right into his hands. He could come at her from the side, from around a corner, even from above, since the lockers didn't go all the way to the ceiling. He could be hiding up there, lying flat in the dark, stretched out across several lockers, ready to leap down and ambush her as she walked by.

Maybe if she stayed by the door and began screaming . . . no, that was too dangerous. He'd know, then, exactly where she was, and maybe no one else would hear her and get there in time to save her.

Better to be quiet, as quiet as death. Breathing softly, she began to inch away from the door, across the tile, being careful not to bump into the shadowy benches or lockers, listening carefully every second for the tiniest of sounds from somewhere else in the room that would confirm what she knew was true: that she wasn't alone.

She heard nothing. But she knew, she knew . . .

So she should have been prepared when it happened. But she wasn't.

She was almost to her locker again when it came from behind, the thing with its prickly, broken strings smashing down over her head and face, scraping the skin as it was mashed roughly downward to settle around her neck, its smooth wooden handle turned toward the back so that her attacker could pull and tug on it, dragging her backward across the tile.

She was too startled, and then too terrified, to scream. Her hands went to her throat to pull the painful, scratching, splintered strings away, but he was pulling on it too hard from behind. The soft skin of her throat hurt terribly, and the wooden frame of the racket was digging into her windpipe, making it difficult to breathe.

"A nice, empty locker," a voice behind her breathed close to her right ear, "let's find us a nice, empty locker."

She didn't recognize the voice. But she was so frightened, she didn't think she would recognize her own mother's voice. "You're hurting me," she whispered. "It hurts." Her fingers clutched at the wooden rim of the racket, but she couldn't pull it away from her throat. He was pulling on it too tightly. "Stop, please stop!"

He didn't answer. The locker door squeaked as he pulled it open.

She knew instantly, with a terribly sinking of her heart, whose locker it was. She had seen

Barb walk over to it dozens of times, reach in and take out shampoo or a towel.

Of course, it was empty now.

Nicki struggled, trying to kick out behind her. But the rim of the racket around her neck was diminishing her oxygen supply. Red and orange spots lit up the darkness, and her body was beginning to feel sluggish, as if she'd just awakened from a long sleep.

"You do know," the hoarse, low voice behind her whispered ominously, "that there won't be enough air in this locker to keep you going all night. I've fixed that. But then, that's the way the tennis ball bounces, right?"

"Why?" Nicki gasped, still struggling, "why?"

"Because of what you did," came the harsh, angry answer. "But you're not going to get away with it."

"I'm sorry!" Nicki cried. The more she struggled, the deeper the splintered strings cut into her skin. "I didn't mean it."

"Maybe not, but you didn't *care*, either. That's what I can't forgive you for. You didn't *care*, Nicole."

She never saw his face. He stayed behind her. Wrapping one arm around her waist to keep her in place, he yanked the racket off her head. Then, as she hungrily gulped in fresh air, he grabbed her damp hair, and with a grasp stronger than she would have imagined possible for any human being, lifted her up and thrust her, face first, into the locker.

The top shelf, on which they all put their make-up kits and hairdryers, had been removed, making it possible for her to stand up straight, her face pressed into the cold metal back of the narrow cubicle.

Although her mind was numb with fear and shock, some small area of her brain was still alert enough to know that the door to the locker mustn't close. It. Must. Not. If it closed, and no one came to let her out until morning, she could die.

If he hadn't paused to gloat, she would have had no chance at all.

"You should've died. But then I was just going to blind you," the voice whispered behind her. "I thought that would be fair after all. Just to take something valuable from you, like you did to me. But the paint thinner didn't do what I wanted it to. I didn't put enough of it in the paint. This is better, anyway. You'll have all night to think about what you've done. And by the time someone finds you, you won't be thinking at all. I'm going to close the door now, Nicki. Nightie-night! Sleep tight, don't let the bedbugs bite."

Years of racing around tennis courts had given Nicki strong leg muscles. Now that the tennis racket wasn't cutting off her air supply, she didn't feel quite as weak. Still, she forced herself to wait until, while he was still talking, she heard the squeak of the locker door closing. Then she kicked backward with her left leg, her sneakered foot slamming into the door with all the force of a mule's kick. She connected just as the door was about to close. He had to have been standing directly behind it, because when it flew backward in response to her kick, a pained shout told her the door had hit its target.

Nicki whirled, jumping from the locker and running down the aisle without stopping to see who was behind the door.

Ignoring the infuriated cursing behind her, she raced around a corner and there it was. A back door. If it was locked, she was dead. If he'd been angry at her before, he'd be a lot angrier now. He was shouting her name now, sounding wild with fury. If he caught her . . .

The door was unlocked.

Nicki yanked it open, and ran for her life.

Chapter 16

Nicki ran blindly, out of the locker room, out of the dome, out into a cold, dark night, legs pumping, arms waving wildly. Her throat throbbed painfully, and when she put a hand up, her fingers came away sticky. The jagged, cut strings had left deep, bloody scratches.

Had he followed? Was he behind her, maybe only steps away? How hard had the locker door slammed into him?

She didn't know where to go. To her room? Would she be safe there? Or to the security guard office, to gasp out her story and get help?

Nicki looked around wildly. Help. She needed help. Where . . . where to get it?

Too frightened to think clearly, she kept running, staying close to the protection of buildings, until she reached, without thought, the security office. She hadn't even known she was headed in that direction.

It was closed. The lights inside were on, but when she tried the doorknob, it didn't turn. Locked. Office empty, door locked. Out on an emergency, maybe.

Freezing . . . hadn't grabbed her jacket . . . no gloves, and her hair was still wet. Pneumonia, her mother would say, "You're going to get pneumonia."

Better to die of pneumonia in a nice, clean hospital bed than to suffocate in a dark, narrow, metal locker.

She wasn't safe out here. She had to find safety.

She whirled away from the empty office, and raced back to Devereaux, to her room where she slammed and locked the door and, for added measure, thrust her desk chair up underneath the doorknob.

Then she hurried to her bed and collapsed on the bedspread.

Of course he knew where she lived. Had to. He'd hung the racket from the ceiling. But if he came now, he wouldn't be able to get in. She was safe, for the moment.

She should call someone. But who? Who was it exactly that she trusted at this moment? Who did she know who would never, never have entered the locker room, hidden until the door was locked, and then attacked her?

She couldn't be sure. Anyone could have done that. Anyone.

The phone rang.

She stared at it.

It rang again.

She reached out and picked it up, but said nothing.

"Nicki?" Deacon's voice. "Nicki, is that you? Where have you been? I've been calling. You were supposed to meet Mel and me, remember? At Vinnie's. Have you seen her?"

Nicki had forgotten. She remembered now. Deacon and Mel had been complaining that she'd been spending too much time with "the tennis crowd," so she'd promised to have dinner with them tonight. She'd forgotten, even before she stepped into the shower. No wonder they were both angry with her.

"Have I seen Mel? No. Isn't she with you?"

"Nicki. If Mel were with me, would I be asking if you'd seen her?"

Nicki almost responded angrily, "How can I be expected to think clearly after what I've been through?" She bit the words back because . . . because why? Because she couldn't be sure that Deacon, nice, funny, Deacon, hadn't been in that locker room with her. Couldn't. Be. Sure.

"Sorry. But I haven't seen her. Maybe she's

at the library." That, too, was a dumb thing to say. Mel only went to the library to pore over art books, and she didn't do that very often. She preferred to "come up with my own ideas; that way I know they're totally original."

"She's not at the library. And she's not in her room, and no one's seen her."

"You sound . . . worried." That seemed silly to Nicki. If anyone could take care of herself, Melanie Hayden could. It was Nicki Bledsoe that Deacon should be worried about.

"I *am* worried. Mel gets in these moods . . ."

"She's an artist. She's supposed to be moody. Comes with the territory, doesn't it?"

Deacon sighed impatiently. "I mean *real* moods, Nicki. When she won't talk and she doesn't sleep and she can't eat. She goes off by herself and broods, sometimes for days at a time. Doesn't care about school, doesn't care about anything. I don't like it, and I think that might be what she's doing now."

"Why does she do it?" Nicki asked bluntly. She had almost been killed tonight, and here came Deacon, expecting her to be as worried as he was about a high-strung, melodramatic friend. She just didn't have the emotional energy to spend on Mel.

"She never said. Hinted that something happened to her a long time ago, but never gave me the details. Said it gets to her sometimes, and she can't stand it, so she hides out to deal with it."

Nicki's heart turned over. Something had happened to Mel a long time ago?

Mel didn't play tennis. She had said she never had. But she might have lied. If she was a murderer, lying would be a piece of cake. And she *had* turned completely around in the hall that night when Deacon called her name. As if she wasn't able to simply glance over her shoulder.

"Where is she from?" Nicki asked. "Where did Mel go to high school?"

"In New Jersey. Fairlawn. Why?"

New Jersey. So if Mel had played tennis when she was twelve, and if she was any good, she could have been in the Tri-State tournament that year. And it could have been Mel who talked Deacon into making friends with Nicole Bledsoe. Maybe Melanie was her middle name, and her first name was really Theresa. Last name, Gideon. She'd changed it, of course.

"Help me look for her?" Deacon asked.

Oh, god, she couldn't, not now, not tonight. She still hadn't done anything about the brutal scratches and cuts on her neck from the splintered tennis racket strings. And she should call security and tell them what had happened.

But something kept her from telling Deacon the whole story. If Mel was the adult Gideon child, Deacon could be in on the plan for revenge, too.

In fact, Nicki thought, her eyes widening, maybe this phone call was a trap. Maybe Mel had put him up to it. Mel could be standing right there with Deacon, listening to see if Nicki fell for the ruse.

"I'm sorry, Deacon," she said stiffly, "but I can't help you out now. I'm not feeling very well. I'm sure Mel's fine. She can take care of herself."

There was a long silence on the other end of the line. "You're not going to help me look for her?" he asked, sounding stunned. "Nicki, Mel is *missing*."

"You don't know that. You said yourself that she likes to go off alone. Hasn't she always surfaced after a while?"

"Yes, but . . ."

"There, you see! She'll pop up any minute." If she hasn't already, Nicki thought angrily.

Another silence, and then Deacon said in a cold voice, "Sorry I bothered you. You must be exhausted after hours of hitting tennis balls across a net. Sleep well."

The click of his receiver hanging up was even colder than his voice.

The conversation left Nicki very uneasy. On the one hand, if Deacon had been laying a trap for her, wouldn't he have insisted more strongly that she join him? He wouldn't have given up so easily, would he?

Unless . . . hadn't she just told him exactly where she was and that she wasn't planning on leaving? She'd practically handed him an engraved invitation. Maybe that was why he'd given up so easily. He and Mel could be on their way over right now.

Nicki jumped off the bed, grabbed her sleeping bag out of the closet, and ran from the room.

She went upstairs to Pat and Ginnie's room, praying as she took the fire stairs two at a time that they'd be there.

They were. Pat was in her robe, studying at her desk, and Ginnie was in bed, reading.

"Nicki!" Pat cried when Nicki burst in without knocking, "what's wrong? And what on earth happened to your neck?"

"Lock the door," Nicki said curtly, hurrying over to sit down on Pat's bed. She told them, quickly and breathlessly, what had happened. She had just reached the part about the security guard's office being empty when Ginnie leaned forward, into the light, and Nicki noticed with shock the bruise on her face. It was new, just beginning to swell, and covered half her left cheek.

Nicki broke off her story to say, "Ginnie, what happened to your face?"

Ginnie laughed self-consciously, reaching up to gently touch her purplish cheek. "Nothing as dramatic as what happened to you. No big deal. Go on with your story."

"No. I *want* to hear what happened to you." And suddenly, Nicki very much wanted to hear what had happened to Ginnie's face. Because that bruise on her cheek looked like it could very easily have been made by a metal door slamming backward into her face.

"Well," Ginnie said, her hand gently rubbing the bruise, "you won't believe this, but I fell. I just fell. When we got to the mall, John said he was too busy to go eat. He said maybe later, so I decided to shop while I was waiting for him, but Pat didn't want to, so she went back to campus. When I went to the candy store to buy some jelly beans, I slipped on something gooey and fell, like someone in a cartoon. It really hurt when my cheek slapped against the tile. So I decided not to wait for John. I just came home. But that's nothing compared to what happened to you, Nicki. Are you okay?"

Nicki was quiet for a moment studying Ginnie. Had she really fallen at the mall? . . .

Maybe she hadn't. And maybe her name wasn't really Ginnie. Maybe it was Teresa Virginia Gideon.

No, that couldn't be. Because Ginnie played tennis. So she couldn't possibly have only partial vision. How could she keep track of the ball if she only had sight in one eye?

She couldn't. Ridiculous to even think it.

Nicki had never been so tired in her life. Tired of trying to figure things out, tired of being scared, tired of not trusting anyone. All she wanted to do was sleep and sleep and sleep.

But first, she called security.

The security guard kept them up for a long time, asking questions.

When he was finished, promising to check out the locker room, they all fell into an exhausted sleep.

Nicki dreamed that she was lying on her back in a long, cold, metal box with a door that wouldn't open no matter how hard she kicked and pounded against it.

Her legs were still thrashing violently in her sleeping bag when she awoke, drenched with cold sweat, late the following morning.

Chapter 17

Pat and Ginnie had already left when Nicki awoke. The cluttered, sunny room was empty, and she felt a sudden pang of abandonment. Sunny or not, daylight or not, she didn't want to be alone.

She wasn't alone for long. She had dressed, and rolled her sleeping bag up into a bundle which she thrust under Ginnie's bed, when a sharp rap on the door halted her movements.

She stood motionless in the middle of the room, unwilling to answer the knock. It might be the security guard . . . but it might not. It didn't have to be dark outside for evil to come knocking at your door. Acts of violence took place during the day, too. If the security guard had been successful in finding the person who had attacked her, she'd have heard by now. He would have called.

No one had.

"Nicki?" It was Deacon.

She didn't answer.

"Mel's back," he said after a few moments of silence. "She was down by the river. Nicki, answer me!"

Now was the time to get some answers. "Did she drive there?" Nicki asked. If Mel drove, if she had a driver's license, she couldn't be Terry Gideon. And that would mean that Deacon wasn't involved, either, wouldn't it? She already knew that he drove, and therefore couldn't possibly have partial vision.

"Mel? Drive?" Deacon laughed. "Mel doesn't drive. She regards cars as the ultimate polluter, although she's perfectly happy to ride in one when she has somewhere to go."

Nicki's heart sank. If Mel was the Gideon child, Deacon almost *had* to be helping her. They were such good friends. How could Mel possibly have done the things she did to Nicki without Deacon knowing?

Neither of them played tennis.

"I'm glad you found Mel," Nicki said, not moving toward the door. "But I have a terrible headache, Deacon. I'm cutting class today. I'll talk to you later, okay?"

His voice was softer, gentler as he said from beyond the door, "Is that a promise? Pat told me what happened last night, Nicki. I don't like it at all. I don't think you should be alone."

What a coincidence, she thought. Neither do I.

But I have to be careful about the company I keep. Very careful.

"I'll wait for you after tennis practice," he said, and then she heard his footsteps moving away, down the hall.

She spent the rest of the day in a dim corner of the library, avoiding the light of day. Whatever she decided to do next, it seemed better to do it under cover of darkness.

She did go to practice, because while the locker room itself was now haunted with the ghost of her attacker, she at least felt safe around the players. All she had to do was make absolutely sure she wasn't left alone for a single second.

Everyone had heard about the incident of the night before, and most of the team seemed genuinely concerned about Nicki's safety. Even Libby said, in passing, "I thought our security was better than that"—although she didn't ask Nicki if she was okay.

Nicki relaxed slowly, and by the end of the session, was playing her best. It was easy to pretend that the ball was her attacker, and slam it back across the net with a fury she'd never before experienced.

As her feet raced back and forth across the court, her mind raced, too.

I didn't mean to hurt anyone when I tossed that racket . . . Wham!

I've been sorry ever since . . . Wham!

I never did anything like that again . . . Wham!

It was a long time ago. It's not fair to come after me now, especially since I didn't even know I hurt anyone . . . Wham, Wham!

"Wow," John said in admiration when she took a break and moved to the sidelines to grab a cup of water, "you've got some arm. Hope you never have to use it against me."

"Scaring you, am I?" she said grimly. "Good! If I look tough, maybe I'll feel tough, and that's what I need right now."

John nodded. "Yeah, I heard. You okay? Security find out anything?"

"Yes, I'm okay, and no, they didn't." Nicki noticed Ginnie watching them from a distance. She wasn't smiling. Nicki wasn't even sure that Ginnie saw them. She seemed to be daydreaming, lost in a fog. "Listen, are you working tonight?" she asked John.

"Sure, Why?"

"Because I need a new racket. I could use your help picking one out."

"No problem. I'll be the only one there tonight. It won't be busy, and I promise I'll devote myself totally to getting you exactly what you need. And deserve," he added with a smile.

"Thanks, John."

"Want me to come with you to the mall tonight?" Pat offered later. "Ginnie will come, too, I'm sure. She pretends she doesn't have time for John, but I know she's interested. This would give her a chance to see him."

Nicki didn't really want to go to the mall alone. Didn't want to go anywhere alone. But she wanted to take her time selecting a racket, and anyone who went with her would get bored waiting, unless they had tons of money to go shopping. Ginnie might, but Pat didn't.

Nicki didn't want to point that out, so she said instead, "No, thanks. John's offered to help me, so I'll be fine. I'll come up to your room when I get back and show you what I got."

Pat grinned. "And if we don't like it, after John-the-expert has helped you pick it out, you'll take it back?"

"No." Nicki returned the grin. "But I'll thank you for your opinion."

"That's what I thought."

Nicki didn't take her shower in the locker room. She pulled sweats on over her whites and hurried from the dome before anyone else.

Deacon was, true to his word, waiting for her outside. He had apparently forgiven her for not helping him look for Mel. Mel wasn't with him.

"Is she still feeling down?" Nicki asked as he walked her back to Devereaux. She was glad to see Deacon, in spite of her doubts about him.

"A little. She had to go to the mall, but she didn't want me along. So I guess she's not ready to rejoin the real world just yet. Soon, though. These moods of hers never last long."

"If I'd known she was going, I'd have asked her to wait for me. I have to go, too. But I guess she wouldn't have wanted my company either, right?"

"Right. I'll drive you, though, if you want."

Alone in a car with Deacon when she couldn't be sure that his good friend Mel wasn't Terry Gideon? Not a good idea.

"Oh, thanks, Deacon," she said easily, "but you'd just be bored."

Deacon frowned. "Well, excuse me. No non-tennis-playing peasants allowed in Nicole Bledsoe's life?"

He sounded angry. Nicki moved away from him. "I've had a lot on my mind lately, Deacon, you know that. Don't start giving me a hard time, okay?"

"Why not?" His voice deepened, became

harsher. "Isn't that what you've been giving me? Maybe it's time to decide who your friends really are, Nicki. Mel was there for you when the tennis crowd didn't want you. Now that she could use some support, where are *you*?"

"You said yourself she didn't want to be around anyone, not even you!" Nicki responded hotly. The accusation seemed unfair. "Why would she want *me* around?"

"Because," he said firmly, "you're a girl. It might be easier for her to talk to you. I know there are a lot of things Mel hasn't told me."

Maybe. Or, maybe Deacon was lying, and Mel *had* told him everything. Every single depressing little thing. In which case, what Deacon was trying to do right now was get Nicki to go searching for Mel at the mall. He could be setting a trap. Maybe the plan was, Nicki would find Mel, and then something terrible would happen to Nicki Bledsoe at the Twin Falls mall. Like something terrible had happened to Barb.

So, ignoring what could either be hurt or anger in Deacon's dark eyes, she said, "I've got to go. Thanks for walking me back. Talk to you later," and hurried inside the dorm.

Chapter 18

There was a note on Nicki's door from the security guard. It read:

> *"Gideon's in Hawaii. Unavailable. But Terry Gideon's former high school says Gideon now student at Salem. Principal there unaware of any name change. Call this office."*

Nicki sagged against the door frame, the note crumpled in her hand. Why hadn't he said what gender the Gideon child was? She *needed* to know that. It was important. At least then she'd know which segment of the student population to completely steer clear of. All girls? Or all boys?

Unless Terry Gideon had a really awesome disguise, she thought wryly.

She called the security office immediately, but got no answer.

She showered, dressed in wool slacks and a heavy sweater and boots, and left the room. Going to the mall might not be safe, but since she couldn't think of any place that was, maybe buying a new tennis racket would at least lift her spirits.

At the last minute, Nicki decided to take the small yellow shuttle bus instead of driving. The thought of walking into a dark parking lot to get her car made her skin crawl. There would be other people on the shuttle bus. She'd be safer there.

During the ride into town, Nicki watched the white, barren landscape float by the windows and thought about leaving Salem. She could go back to State. She wished she could leave right now, tomorrow. She knew the kids there, knew the tennis team, wouldn't have to start all over again. It wasn't as if she'd been at Salem that long. There wouldn't be that awful, painful wrench if she left.

She'd be safe at State.

But for how long? her reflection in the bus window asked her. Someone wants to *kill* you, Nicki. Do you really think he couldn't find you at State? It's not that far away.

Which brought her to another question. Her

acceptance at State had made the sports pages last summer. If Gideon was looking for her, why hadn't he or she looked for her at State instead of waiting until she got to Salem? If you were that full of hate and the need for revenge, wouldn't you go just about anywhere to get satisfaction? Why had her tormentor matriculated at Salem instead of State if he — or she — wanted to get at Nicki Bledsoe? Whoever it was couldn't have known that she'd be transferring to Salem.

Nicki leaned her head wearily against the window. How could she possibly know what was going on in the mind of someone so twisted and sick?

She remembered the note from the security guard. Maybe she'd have some answers soon. Maybe then it would all come to an end.

And she realized then that she didn't want to leave Salem. Yes, arriving had been difficult, playing tennis had been difficult, none of it had been easy. And then the terrible things had started happening. She *should* want to leave.

But she didn't. She just didn't.

John seemed glad to see her when she got to the mall. "It's been really dead," he said. As he led her to the rackets. I've finished restocking the shelves and I even read two chapters of my chem book."

She tested a dozen rackets before coming up with the one that felt right. It wasn't the same brand as her old one, but it was one of the better brands, and when she swung it half a dozen times, testing, she knew it was the one she wanted.

"It's perfect," she said, smiling up at him. "Perfect! Thanks for your help."

"No problem. Need anything else? Socks, shoes, headband, wristband?"

"No, thanks. This was all I wanted."

A couple came in, looking around expectantly.

"You go ahead and wait on them," Nicki urged, still swinging the racket. "I'm going to keep playing around with this, just to make sure. I'm not in any hurry." That was certainly true enough. She felt comfortable there, a feeling that would quickly disappear, she knew, when she left the store.

"Nicki?"

Nicki's arm stopped, mid-swing. Mel's voice, right behind her. "Buying a new racket? I heard what happened to your old one. Too bad."

Nicki turned around. Mel looked pale and tired, with deep, lavender shadows circling her eyes. "Want to grab a cup of coffee? Maybe a slice of pizza? I haven't eaten, and I'm starved."

Had Deacon told Mel that Nicki was going to the mall? He couldn't have called Mel, not at the mall, but she could have called him. Could have said, "Where exactly is it that Nicki was going?" And he could have said, "You'll find her in the sporting-goods store, Mel."

"No, thanks," Nicki said, shaking her head. "I have to pay for this racket, and then I need to go straight back to campus and study. Big test tomorrow in . . . in English." Mel wasn't in her English class. "And I'm really not hungry. Big dinner." Big lie. She'd had no dinner at all.

"Oh, come on, Nicki, please. I've hardly seen you lately. You're so busy with tennis. I . . . I could use someone to talk to. Deacon's great, but sometimes I need a girl to talk to."

Nicki hesitated. Exactly what Deacon had said. What if she was way off-base about the two of them? Besides, Mel looked too exhausted to attack anyone. And even if she wasn't, what could she do to Nicki in the middle of a mall?

If I have coffee with her, maybe I'll find out something useful, Nicki thought. Not knowing is driving me crazy. I can at least ask Mel where she's from. Of course, she could always lie. But maybe not. "Okay. A quick sandwich, in the food court." The food court would have people in it. Which made it safe. "Wait'll I tell John. I'll have him hold this, and come back to pay for it after we've eaten."

"She looks awful," John said in a low voice when Nicki went to the counter to give him the racket. "What's wrong with her?"

"I don't really know. Tell you when I get back. If she tells me."

Mel did tell her. "I had this friend," she said when they had their food and were seated in the food court. She absentmindedly stirred her coffee as she spoke. "Best friend I'd ever had. We met in first grade and were hardly ever apart after that. We were both going to be artists, and we spent hours drawing and painting and even designing clothing we wanted to wear when we were grown-up. Her name was Tabitha. Tabbie. She hated the nickname, said it made her sound like a cat, and insisted that I call her by her full name, or she wouldn't answer me."

"Where did you live when you were a kid?" Nicki couldn't help asking.

"Fairlawn, New Jersey. Little tiny town, not much to do there, but Tab and I kept busy."

Just as Deacon had said. That meant that Mel could have taken part in the Forest Hills Tri-state tournament.

"When we were sixteen, Tabitha started

180

getting really tired, and there always seemed to be bruises on her arms and legs. I knew her parents, knew she wasn't being abused or anything like that, so I knew there was something else wrong." Mel fell silent, her eyes on the table.

"What?" Nicki pressed. "What was it?"

Mel lifted her head, her eyes bleak. "Leukemia. The worst kind. She lived another eight months and five days."

Nicki couldn't think of anything to say. She finally managed, "Mel, I'm so sorry."

Tears of pain filled Mel's eyes. "For a while, I was mad, and I didn't know what I was mad at exactly. Then I finally realized I was really ticked at Tab, for abandoning me. That made me feel guilty, so I just felt worse."

Nicki said nothing. What was there to say?

"I was so sure I would never feel good again," Mel continued. "And then, one spring day in senior year, I did. I just did. So I finished high school and came here, just like Tab and I had planned. I guess one of the reasons I don't have any friends who are girls is because I compare all of them to her. And no one's good enough. So it just seems easier to make friends with guys. But it's hard to tell them everything."

"Deacon doesn't know about Tabitha?"

Mel shook her head.

"You should tell him. I know he'd understand. He can't figure out why you go off the way you do, every once in a while. You should tell him."

Mel nodded. "Maybe I will." She swiped at her eyes with the back of her hand. "Thanks for listening, okay? I needed to talk to someone, and I know I haven't seen much of you lately, but I always thought maybe we could be really good friends."

Nicki felt a flush of shame. She'd been so wrong about Mel. Mel *and* Deacon. And she hadn't been a very good friend. At first, because she'd been so determined to make the tennis team accept her. And then, when most of them had, she'd neglected the two people who didn't care whether or not she played tennis well. Later, she'd avoided them because they *didn't* play the game, and she'd been afraid that meant something sinister. So she hadn't felt safe around them. But she couldn't very well tell Mel that. Not now. Maybe never.

"I'm sorry about your friend," she said quietly. "Any time you want to talk, let me know. I promise you, I'll be around."

And she meant it.

"I feel a lot better," Mel said. "Thanks for listening, Nicki. In fact, I feel so much better that I think I'm going to see if I can dig up that new shade of turquoise that my art teacher said is available now in pastels. It's almost closing time, but we have a few minutes. Meet you at the shuttle if you finish about the same time that I do?"

"Right." Nicki was anxious to pay for her racket and get back to campus, so she could call Deacon and begin mending fences, if possible.

She hurried back to the sporting-goods store. It was almost closing time, but John would wait for her. He knew she was coming back.

John had already turned off most of the lights.

"Sneaking out early?" she teased, walking over to the circular counter in the center of the store. He was standing at the cash register, adding up the day's receipts. She stood beside him, pulling the credit card from her wallet. "Weren't you even going to wait for my money? You must not work on commission." She extended the card, expecting him to reach out and take it.

He didn't. He didn't even seem to see it. He appeared to be completely oblivious of her outstretched arm.

Must be lost in the counting of money, she thought.

"John?" she said inquiringly, "don't you want my money?"

He looked up. But instead of simply glancing to his right side, where she stood, which anyone else would have done, John turned his entire body around to face her. Only then did he see the card, and reach out a hand to take it from her.

Nicki froze. No. Not John. No.

But . . . John had turned completely around before he could see what was at his right side.

John spent much of his free time at the tennis courts, around tennis players, because he loved the game and knew a lot about it.

How could John know so much about the game if he'd never played it?

Maybe he had. Once upon a time.

He would know a lot about tennis if he'd played as a child. Especially if he'd been really good. If he'd had the potential to become a champion.

John?

No.

Yes.

When he returned the card to her, he again turned his body completely around, away from the cash register, instead of just reaching slightly sideways.

Because he couldn't see out of his right eye. Because it had been severely injured six years ago. By a stone tossed up into the air when a racket was thrown to the ground.

Nicki knew with absolute certainty that she was looking at Terry Gideon, all grown-up now.

And blind in one eye.

Chapter 19

Nicki took several steps backward, away from the counter. "You're Terry Gideon," she said in an awe-stricken voice. She moved a few steps away from the counter.

She expected his face to change, to fill with rage or hatred, now that he'd been exposed.

To her astonishment, he first looked startled and then his broad face eased into a grin, and he said, his voice perfectly friendly, "Hey, how'd you know that? I haven't used my real name since I got here."

Puzzled, Nicki stared at him. Why did he still look so friendly? Why wasn't he coming out from behind the counter, intent on finishing the job he'd started in the locker room? "I . . . I just realized that you . . . that you can't see out of your right eye."

His hand instinctively flew up to cover the eye. "Oh, that. Geez, you could tell? And I thought I was doing such a hot job of covering up." He looked at her anxiously. "You're not going to share the news, are you? God, if there's one thing I can't stand, it's pity. Keep it to yourself, okay, Nicki?"

He made no move toward her. The expression on his face remained friendly. His only concern now seemed to be that she might not keep his secret. When, too stunned to speak, she didn't answer, he continued, "That's why I don't use my real name. When people find out I can't see out of one eye, they treat me differently. I hate that. And there was so much publicity in this whole area when the accident happened, I knew there'd be fellow students who might recognize the name, especially the tennis players. I did run into a few people here at Salem who knew me from high school. But they were cool when I explained what I was doing, and they were nice enough not to pass the info around campus." He grinned at her again. "The name seemed kind of appropriate. I mean, Long John Silver was a pirate and wore an eye patch, right?"

When she still didn't say saything, John flushed and said in a different tone of voice, "Nicki, I'd appreciate it if you'd quit staring. You can't tell by looking, anyway. There's nothing to see, nothing to give me away."

"I'm . . . I'm sorry. That's not why I was staring. I was staring because . . . because you're not mad. At me."

John lifted his eyebrows. "What? Why would I be mad at you? That's nuts. I've been stared at worse than that before. There was this group of kids in my tenth-grade social studies class who stared at me constantly, trying to figure out which eye it was."

"No, that's not what I mean. Not for staring. For . . ." Nicki stopped, took a deep breath. If he didn't know, why tell him?

Because she had to.

"You really don't know who I am, do you?" she said, moving back toward the counter.

"Who you are? Sure. You're Nicole Bledsoe, tennis champion. Actually, I think I may have played at Forest Hills with you once, a long time ago." John glanced down at his bulk with amusement. "I looked a lot different then, so I wouldn't expect you to recognize me. When I couldn't play tennis anymore, I started putting on weight. I was actually pretty hefty for a while there, until I got my height."

"I did play in that tournament at Forest Hills," she said quietly, her eyes never leaving his face. "John, I was the one who threw that racket. The racket that tossed those stones up into the air. It's my fault you can't see out of your right eye."

It was his turn to stare. "You're kidding, right?"

"No. I'm not. It was my racket. When I heard you scream, I got scared and ran. I just found out how much damage I'd done. My parents never told me. I didn't know."

When John spoke again, he leaned his elbows on the counter and said, "It was *you?* Wow, this is really weird. I've been following your career all this time . . . I was the one who recommended you to Coach, did you know that?"

Nicki nodded. "She told me."

John kept shaking his head in wonderment. "You threw that racket? This is too bizarre. Your parents paid all my medical bills, did you know that?"

"Yes. I just found out."

"I never knew who they were. Who you were. My parents wouldn't give me the name. They said it wouldn't do me any good to know."

"I thought you knew it was me," Nicki said slowly. "I mean, I thought, Terry Gideon knew it was me. And hated me for it."

"I did hate you. For a while. I never knew if you were a girl or a guy, I only knew you'd ruined my life."

Nicki flushed with shame and guilt.

"But it didn't last," John added hastily, seeing the look on her face. "Actually, I think when it happened I was already burned out on tennis. I'd already started to gain a little weight, puberty, I guess, and it was getting tiring racing around on those courts. I hated you for a while and then I decided it wasn't so bad, having more time to do other things. I found out there were lots of other fun things to do, and that was neat."

Nicki was trying to take it all in. In the space of one hour, she had learned that Mel wasn't, after all, the Gideon child she'd injured, and that John Silver was. But . . . John wasn't acting as if he hated her and wanted her dead.

Then . . . who *did*?

She'd thought she had it all figured out.

Wrong.

"You really don't hate me?" she asked tentatively.

"Did you continue to throw your racket when you lost a match?" he asked, smiling.

"No. Never after that night."

"Then I don't hate you." Then he added more seriously, "Look, Nicki, we were *twelve years old*. We were *kids*. I've had a lot of time to think about it, and I finally decided that the person who threw that racket down never intended to blind anyone, not even partially. I could have done the same thing. I was pretty frustrated by then, and was tempted more than once to bean an opponent with a well-placed racket."

She had one more thing to say. "John? I only just found out what I did. And now that I know, I want to tell you that I'm sorrier than I can say. I'm glad you don't hate me, but that doesn't change the fact that I wish I had never let go of that racket. I'm sorry I hurt you."

"Apology accepted," he said lightly. "Listen, I've got to close this place up, or security is going to think there's a robbery in progress. Wait while I put the money away and deal with the rest of the lights, and then we'll go back to school on the shuttle together, okay? I'll lock up. We can go out the back way, from the office." He frowned again. "I heard about what happened last night. You shouldn't be going anywhere alone." He picked up the cash drawer and looked at her. "Oh, geez, I just got it. You thought that was *me*, in the locker room? Trying to wipe you off the face of the earth?"

"Not *you*. Not John Silver. Terry Gideon. But I didn't know if Terry Gideon was a girl or a guy. I . . . I thought it might be Mel. She's been acting weird lately. But I found out why tonight, and then I knew it wasn't her."

John paused, reading her thoughts. "So . . . if it wasn't Mel slamming that tennis racket over your head, and it wasn't Terry Gideon . . . me . . . then . . . who do you think it was?"

Nicki groaned. "Oh, God, I don't know. I don't have any idea. I was so sure it was Terry Gideon, that I never even thought about anyone else."

John walked to the front of the store to close and lock the doors, then came back to lead the way to the office where he had to deposit the cash drawer. They began walking to the rear of the store. John hit light switches as they went and the huge space behind them disappeared into darkness. But the light in the office was on, guiding their way.

"If it wasn't you," she said thoughtfully, "if it wasn't Terry Gideon, who had every reason to hate me, then I don't know who it was. Because I don't know anyone else who hates me. The voice in the doorway at the infirmary said I'd taken something from them. When I found out about you, I figured that meant taking away the sight in your eye. That made sense. I don't know what else I've taken from someone."

"Well, there's the scholarship," John said, opening the office door and carrying the cash drawer to a small safe squatting against one wall opposite the back door. He knelt to open the safe.

Nicki, standing in the doorway, thought she heard a sound behind them, in the darkened store. She turned to look, but could see nothing. And her mind was on John's surprising comment. "Scholarship? What scholarship?"

"The full tennis scholarship. They only give three. The rest are partials. Libby has one and a guy named Ty has one, and that leaves yours. Which belonged to someone else first semester. I know, because when I recommended you to Coach after seeing you play at State, she said the only way she could offer you a full was if she took it away from someone else. After she saw you, she told me that's what she'd decided to do. She was going to take it from someone who hadn't been playing all that well."

"She took a scholarship away from someone else to give it to me?" Nicki was horrified. No one had told her that. *"Who?"*

John put the cash drawer in the safe. "She wouldn't tell me that, and I wouldn't have asked. None of my business. Look, don't start feeling guilty. She said she was going to see that they got a partial. That's better than nothing, right? Some players don't even have that."

Nicki heard the noise again, a rustling sound

from behind her left shoulder. "There isn't anyone else in here, is there?" she asked nervously, glancing around again. It was impossible to see anything beyond the office.

"No. Relax. I'll be done here in a minute. We were talking while I was tallying up the receipts and I see an error here. Hold on a sec." He reached up to grab a pencil off the desk, bent his head back to the papers in his hand, and began erasing furiously.

So he didn't see the rear door open.

He didn't see what came through it . . . bulky and burly, wearing a hockey uniform complete with enormous knee and elbow pads and a white molded hockey mask on its face. It lumbered into the room and in three, rolling, awkward strides crossed to where John knelt. In one swift, sure stroke, it brought the hockey stick in its right hand down upon John's head.

There was a sharp, cracking sound, and John crumpled silently to the floor.

The hockey mask turned. Eyes behind the narrow slits stared at Nicki, standing paralyzed in the doorway, her mouth open. Then it came for her.

Chapter 20

Nicki froze. She couldn't think. Couldn't breathe. Her mind raced, but shock had puddled it into a mass of confusion. Then her instincts took over.

Run.

But where? Where could she run to? The front door was locked, the keys on John's belt. The monster in the white mask stood between her and John, making it impossible for her to reach the keys or the only other way out, the rear door of the office.

She could only run in one direction. Back into the store, dark now and filled with shadows of mannequins and shelves and clothing racks and equipment displays.

"Get away from me!" Nicki hissed as the white mask advanced toward her. "Stay away from me!" She whirled and ran.

An alarm, she thought wildly, this is a store,

it must have an alarm, something behind the counter to trip if burglars come, something to summon the police.

She had no idea what an alarm looked like.

But because it was the only hope she had, she ran as fast as the darkness allowed to where she thought the counter should be.

"Nicki," a voice behind her whispered, "there isn't any point in running. The score is forty-love, my favor. I lost to you once. But I'm winning this match. I'll get my scholarship back. I'll stay in school."

Nicki slammed into the counter, wincing as her hip felt the jolt. She rounded the white formica counter and crouched down behind it. A tennis player . . . John had been right, it was a tennis player, after all. She almost laughed, bitterly, aloud. From the moment she'd created a scenario that starred as its villain the injured Gideon child, she had thought she was safe only with tennis players.

And all the time, it was one of them.

How could she have been so wrong?

It had seemed to make perfect sense at the time. But then, she hadn't known about the scholarship.

Footsteps thudded across the carpet toward the counter.

Nicki groped along the underside of the counter for something, anything, that might feel like a silent alarm. A wire? A cord? A button?

The footsteps stopped. "Nick-ee! Oh, Nick-ee, come out, come out, wherever you are! Admit defeat, like a good champion. Not pouting, are we? That's not very sporting of you, Nicole."

The footsteps came closer. Nicki couldn't stay where she was.

Closer. If she did, whoever it was would make her head into a hockey puck, just as he had John's.

John. Was he still alive?

Rage welled up inside Nicki's chest. John hadn't done anything to anyone. John was a good guy. Even though he had plenty of reason to be bitter and hateful, he wasn't.

She wasn't going to let whoever it was win. John needed help. He needed *her*, alive and in one piece.

On her hands and knees, Nicki began to crawl out from behind the counter. The store was full of things that could be used to defend herself. If she could find, in the dark, the hockey equipment, she could arm herself with her own stick. Then she could fight on equal terms. If she couldn't find the hockey sticks, then maybe a baseball bat, a ski, something. . . .

John needed her.

She heard the hockey stick clattering back and forth from one side of the counter to the other, searching for her. She moved faster. She scrambled along the floor, keeping her breathing as quiet as possible, struggling not to bump into a mannequin or a display.

Let me find something, she begged, please, let me find something!

"Nick-ee! Where did you go? Are we playing hide-and-seek now? I don't know that game. My game is tennis, you know. At least, it was until *you* came along. I can't finish school without my scholarship. We had money, once, but my father gambled it all away — everything except my tennis racket."

The top of Nicki's head hit something . . . a leg . . . a leg in ski pants . . . a mannequin's leg in ski pants, and when she lifted her head to look, light reflected from out in the mall shone on the sharp, pointed tip of a ski pole. In the mannequin's hand.

She would have to stand up to remove it from the plaster fingers.

If she stood up, her hunter might see her.

But at least she'd have something to fight with.

"Nick-ee! Give it up. It's over. Forty-love, I told you. You're going to go back to the office with me, and you're going to have an accident back there. John found out who you were, hated you for what you'd done to him, and attacked you with a hockey stick. You fought back, hitting him. But he delivered the final, fatal blow to your skull before passing out himself. Perfect. Don't you think it's perfect? I had planned to make it look like a robbery. But while I was dressing in this monkey suit, I heard you talking to John. Isn't it weird that none of us knew about his eye? But this is so great. He has a reason to hate you, too. And," the voice lifted lightly, "maybe I'll just help myself to some of that money lying there beside John. Not all of it, of course. Now that it's not going to look like a robbery, I'll have to just take a little." The voice hardened again, "I deserve it all, after what you did to me."

Holding her breath, Nicki slowly, cautiously, lifted herself from the floor, trying desperately to remain in the mannequin's shadow, away from the reflected light.

"Maybe," the voice said dreamily, and now

it was moving closer again "maybe I'll buy a nice, new outfit. I could use a new outfit. Something stunning."

"Stunning" was a word Libby would use. Was it Libby, after all? Was it Libby's scholarship Coach had handed over to Nicki? John had said, "Libby has one, and a guy named Ty." But Coach hadn't told him whose scholarship she'd reduced to partial, so it could have been Libby's.

Nicki reached out toward the ski pole, hoping it was settled loosely in the grasp of the mannequin skier, so that she could easily lift it from between the fingers.

"Everything we had was gone. The house, cars, all of my college money. My mother said I'd have to stay home and get a job to help out, but I wouldn't. I wasn't giving up college. Then I'd have to live like *them*, for the rest of my life. No, thanks. I knew I could get a tennis scholarship, and I was right. And when I first got here, I did great. Great at practice, won most of my matches. Coach was pleased. But money was such a problem. There was never enough, never, and the stress of constantly writing home and begging for money got to me. I started screwing up, and losing. I knew Coach was getting impatient with me, but I never thought she'd reduce my scholarship. And she wouldn't have, if it hadn't been for you."

Nicki reached up and tugged on the ski pole. It slid upward easily, and she heaved a sigh of relief.

"I'm getting tired of this game." There was anger in the voice again. "I need my rest. Practice tomorrow, you know. And you won't be there. Everyone will be very upset, saying how awful it is about you and John. Come out now, Nicki, and quit wasting my time."

Nicki continued to slide the ski pole up, up, out of the mannequin's fingers. In just a few seconds now, she'd have it in her hands, and would no longer be defenseless.

Halfway up, the ski pole stuck.

Biting down hard on her lower lip to keep from screaming, Nicki yanked harder on the pole. The mannequin shook, and the ski goggles hanging around its neck clinked noisily, a sound that stopped Nicki's heart as it echoed like a shout throughout the silent store.

"Aha! There you are! Taking up skiing now, are we? You'll never get out on the slopes. Ready or not, here I come!"

The bulky, padded figure in the white hockey mask took off across the carpet, hockey stick raised ominously in the air, heading straight for Nicki. When it was only a few feet away,

"She wasn't all that important, Nicki. She wasn't even that good a tennis player.

"It wasn't my fault," Pat continued. "The only way to get my scholarship back was to get rid of you. Permanently. I *had* to do that, Nicki. It wasn't my fault that was Barb in the tub, and not you."

"I didn't know I'd taken your scholarship," Nicki said, trying to buy some time. "I just found out. Is that why everyone was so cold to me when I arrived?" She began to slide upward, a fraction of an inch at a time.

Pat laughed bitterly. "Not exactly. They didn't know Coach had taken me into her office and explained, oh, so sweetly, that I wasn't living up to my potential and she was very, very sorry, but she had no choice, she would have to reduce my scholarship to a partial. John was the only person Coach told. But I knew. And I spread a rumor that you demanded a full-tuition scholarship, that you wouldn't come to Salem without it. That made you sound greedy and spoiled. So everyone was already against you before you even arrived. Of course, no one knows it was me who spread the rumor. Not even Ginnie. I made sure of that."

If she moved any closer, she would see Nicki's hand pulling the ski pole upward.

"Ginnie had that bruise on her face," Nicki

said. "The night you attacked me in the locker room. Why didn't you have any bruises?"

"I did. On my left shoulder. That's where the door caught me, knocking me off balance."

"You tried to blind me."

"It almost worked. Too bad it didn't."

The pole continued to slide upward, upward . . . almost free of the mannequin's grip.

"Well, it's going to work this time," Pat said emphatically. "The game is over. I think you'll agree that the match goes to me. Winner," she declared, lifting the hockey stick higher and drawing it back behind her head, "and still champion, Patrice Weylen!"

"No!" Nicki shouted, and with one last vigorous yank, pulled the ski pole free. She thrust it out in front of her, its sharp, pointed tip forward.

But Pat was wearing thick layers of padding. The pole wouldn't do any good unless it was thrust into her face. Nicki couldn't do it. She wasn't going to risk blinding another person, not even to save her own life.

Desperately, Nicki raised the ski pole and swung it sideways with all her might even as the hockey stick sliced through the air toward her.

Her blow landed first. It hit Pat's left shoulder, knocking her off balance and deflecting the hockey stick so that it only glanced off Nicki's right arm. Pat staggered sideways in her unwieldy uniform. She dropped the hockey stick and fought to regain her balance, to no avail. As she tilted precariously, her flailing arms struck the mannequin. It tipped, leaned, and toppled forward onto her, knocking her to the ground.

Nicki dropped the ski pole and began backing away, one hand to her mouth.

Sirens sounded startlingly close by. The door burst open. The lights came on.

"Hold it right there," said an official voice.

"Nicki?" a voice called from the office doorway.

Nicki looked up. John, hanging onto the office door for support, said weakly, "I called the police."

As the police led Pat away, she stopped to look at Nicki. She whispered, "You're going to win, after all, aren't you? It wasn't supposed to be like that."

Nicki, sagging against the wall nodded silently.

She *had* won.

She was still alive.

Epilogue

The dome reverberated with the unmistakable sound of tennis balls being whacked back and forth across the nets on every court. A brilliant winter sun shone in through the glass roof, dappling the white-clad players with dancing shadows.

Nicki, breathing hard, took a break. New racket in hand, she ran to the sidelines where Deacon and Mel, John and Ginnie were seated.

"Lookin' good!" Deacon said with a smile. He reached out to take her hand.

"Yeah, not bad," Nicki agreed. A shadow crossed her face. "I guess I play better when the only danger facing me is losing a game, as opposed to losing my *life*." She glanced around the dome, her eyes regretful. "I still can't believe it was Pat. She seemed like such a good friend when hardly anyone else did. I slept in her *room*."

"It was my room, too," Ginnie said. "She wouldn't have done anything to you with me there." The bruise on her face from her fall at the mall had healed completely. She looked healthy and well-rested. Her left hand, Nicki noticed, was firmly ensconced in one of John's. "Anyway, you taught me something. That life is short. Too short to focus on only one thing." She smiled at John. "Right?"

"Right!"

"Well, that's great," Nicki said, sitting down between Deacon and Mel, "because I wouldn't want one of my new roomies to be a tennis nut. Strange things happen to people who become obsessed."

Ginnie had said, "I could never sleep in that room again," and since Nicki felt exactly the same way about her own room, she and Ginnie had both moved out and were now sharing a larger room with Mel.

They had spent that last long night talking about Pat and about what had happened, and when they were finished, they had made a pact not to bring it up again. "We've dissected the whole thing," Nicki had said resolutely, "and we need to put it behind us and get on with other things."

Now, as she sat contentedly between Deacon and Mel, watching Salem's tennis team running around the courts serving and backhanding and smashing the balls across the nets, she realized that was exactly what they'd done.

They'd put the whole horrible business behind them.

Exactly where it belonged.

And if she sometimes imagined Pat's face looking up at her, whispering, "You won . . .", she knew that in time, that, too, would disappear.

"Bledsoe!" Coach yelled, "get out here!"

Nicki jumped up and ran out onto the court.

About the Author

"Writing tales of horror makes it hard to convince people that I'm a nice, gentle person," says **Diane Hoh**.

"So what's a nice woman like me doing scaring people?

"Discovering the fearful side of life: what makes the heart pound, the adrenaline flow, the breath catch in the throat. And hoping always that the reader is having a frightfully good time, too."

Diane Hoh grew up in Warren, Pennsylvania. Since then, she has lived in New York, Colorado, and North Carolina, before settling in Austin, Texas. "Reading and writing take up most of my life," says Hoh, "along with family, music, and gardening." Her other horror novels include *Funhouse*, *The Accident*, *The Invitation*, *The Fever*, and *The Train*.

Return to Nightmare Hall
if you dare . . .

The Coffin

Air.

I need air.

Every time they put me in this dark, narrow, airless space, they insist, as I struggle and scream in fury at them, that there is plenty of air.

But they lie.

It is always the same. In only minutes, my chest begins to ache, as if giant claws are squeezing it. My head hurts as my lungs struggle to pull in enough oxygen. I feel dizzy, as if I've been spinning in circles for hours.

But I haven't been. Because there isn't enough room in my dark, musty chamber to spin, or even to walk. Not enough room to take two steps forward or two steps backward. No room to lie down, and sitting is almost impossible in this tall, dark, narrow, box, unless you scrunch up your legs so that your knees are *jabbing into your stomach like cattle prods. A very painful position, and those times when I've been forgotten in here and had been sitting like that, I was totally unable to walk when they finally remembered and came to let me out. My legs had frozen in their folded-up position. They had to reach in and lift me out. I'm not exactly lightweight, and they had a hard time. That made them mad. But it was their fault for forgetting me.*

Dark. It is so completely black, as if I'd suddenly gone blind. There are no windows in my box, not so much as a tiny crack to let in a sliver of light from the hall outside. And it is quiet, deathly quiet. The wood is thick. Only the loudest sounds penetrate, sounding vague and distant, as if my ears were stuffed with cotton. Faint voices, an unrecognizable note or two of music, occasional muffled footsteps. This place is almost soundproof.

Which makes it as lonely as an isolated mountaintop in Tibet, or the very depths of an ocean, unoccupied by even the bravest of sea creatures.

The sense of isolation is unbearable.

But that's their goal, isn't it? To make it unbearable.

They've succeeded.

It stinks in here, too. The smell of human

panic is everywhere, oozing from the gray-brown boards. Some of the smell is probably mine, past and present.

Once . . . maybe it was the first time they locked me in here . . . I broke every fingernail, ripped them to shreds, trying to claw my way out. And once . . . maybe that was the first time, I had no voice left when they finally set me free. Couldn't talk above a whisper for three days, from the shouting and screaming to be let out.

I won't forget this. It won't be forgiven. Ever. It should never have happened to me. I didn't deserve it. It wasn't necessary.

Never again. I've learned my lesson, here in my dark, silent, torture chamber. Trust is for fools. I will never be that foolish again. Never.

I won't always be trapped in this small, airless hellhole. I'll be free soon. Free to go about my business.

The business of getting even. Payback time.

I know exactly how to go about it. I have a plan. A wonderful plan. Thinking about carrying it out it has kept me from going insane in this loathsome place.

But first, I have to get out. I have to be freed from this medieval nightmare. This obscene box.

This coffin.

NIGHTMARE HALL
where college is a
scream!